MASTERWORKS

and other stories

by Simon Jacobs

instar books • new york

Cover art by Odilon Redon
Cover design by Jeanne Thornton
Interior illustrations by Simon Jacobs

ISBN (paper) 978-1-68219-905-3
ISBN (ebook) 978-1-68219-906-0

Some stories in this book originally appeared, in slightly different forms, in *Joyland*, *Tin House, SmokeLong Quarterly,* and *Paper Darts*.

Distributed to the trade by Small Press Distribution: http://spbooks.org.

Printed in the United States of America
First Printing

For my brothers—

CONTENTS

LET ME TAKE YOU TO OLIVE GARDEN

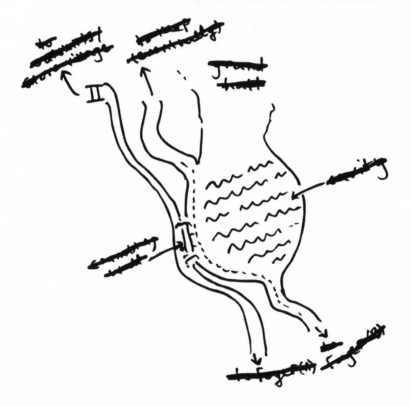

I.

THE YEAR IS 2004. I just got my ears pierced! Reese is wearing eight million bracelets and boots that come up past her knees, so in order to sit in the booth she has to lower herself onto the seat first and then swing her legs rigid under the table. I think that if I ask about each of these bracelets in turn, I will be able to carry our conversation at least through this dinner and possibly into infinity, that we could be talking forever. Instead, because I've been thinking about it, I ask if she thinks the guitar sound in Rise Against's latest album makes them sound too much like a stadium rock band.

Reese juts her head forward and says "What?" And in the tone I detect that it's less a "What?" of indignation at my bold claim and more of a "What?" like she did not take meaning from any of my words. Fortunately, the waiter arrives, and I make it about the breadsticks.

"That's the reason to come to an Olive Garden," I say, looking conspiratorially from the waiter to my date. "Unlimited breadsticks."

Yet when she sits back in the booth, Diet Coke ordered, I decide that Reese is a half-breadstick girl at most, and bizarrely, it still seems to be my turn to ask a question. That said, my capacity is honestly endless; between us, I picture a giant grid, like a mega-calendar, the building blocks of our Great Love, and each blank box comprises a question, and the boxes are filled with bracelets. I imagine checking one off as I open my yap yet again: "Where did you get those bracelets?"

The grid falls to pieces. I've made a terrible mistake, delivered the question totally wrong, in plural—like trying to fan a candle flame by setting the room on fire—and I know the answer before it's delivered: vague, all-encompassing, unparseable, probably two words at most, hacking off the conversation as if with a machete, and now—

Our waiter puts a wire and paper basket of seasoned breadsticks on the table. He drifts off into the restaurant. I should never have mentioned them. The sound outside of our table seems to fade. Reese looks shyly down and begins sliding the bracelets up and down on her wrist, smiling to herself, as if each one is a distinct sensory memory too private to share. "Well, this one comes from Forever 21, this one comes from Claire's, this one comes from JC Penney…"

Her word choice is strangely passive, and as she moves obsessively down her forearm cataloguing every shitty clothing and accessory chain in southern Ohio, I am of two minds. The jangling overcomes everything; her Diet Coke hisses across the table. Motion, thought slows to a crawl. Either she is victim to the most boring and compulsive gifter known to man, or she is a taker.

"Did you *steal* all of those?"

She looks up at me from across the table, her fingers playing with the chain between two sprigs of a charm bracelet. Her eyes look out in a sly drawl, and the breadsticks rise between us like a yeasty monument from before time. Their seasonal glaze dissipates into the heavy air.

But before she can confirm or deny, the ground breaks open to the right of our table, and in the next second the restaurant seems to have doubled its proportions, the kitchen is now a football field away from us, and everything between it and our table has been consumed. The high- and low-calorie vessels move trancelike down our table, and Reese and I reach across and fasten arms in a power grip, like we're bracing for the first drop on a rollercoaster. We jump from the booth at the same time, but Reese's legs are still locked in their great boots beneath the table, so instead of clearing the area she wrenches from my sweaty hands and snaps cleanly mid-thigh, and I watch her tumble along with the entire booth—still positioned as if she's sitting within it, freeze-framed in profile—into the widening chasm now bearing up at me: a gaping, wet cave winding down and out of sight, its walls the same texture and color as the roof of a burned mouth. Everything in the restaurant ricochets into its depths, the patrons breaking apart on the rocks and gradually slopping down the tunnel to join the mound of bodies and wreckage at the juncture where the cave wraps out of sight, like waterlogged meat in a kitchen drain awaiting disposal. I see smaller passages branching out from the tunnel, and some kind of lithe and speckled creatures flit in and out, their skin like leopard print, always just momentarily visible, snatching at the falling humans as they roll past, dragging them whole or piecemeal into their caves. A faint light flickers out as if from a campfire, deep below and out of sight. Screams waft up from beneath me like a song on the wind, and with them, swarming my nostrils, the exact smell of my hands after I've masturbated at the end of an active day, earthy shame

11

and empty potential. And across the gulf now eating into the kitchen on the opposite side, crumbling at my feet on this one, as my heart leaps into my throat with the sudden plunge, I find another: a woman hangs there, her arms planted on the stainless steel counter behind her, legs dangling into the crevasse, emitting the same scream over and over, like a car alarm.

II.

Molly has been upset since her dad died six years ago, fundamentally upset, but tonight she is going to turn it all around. When she enters the LaRosa's Pizzeria ten minutes early and sees Megan already at a booth in the far corner, her hands wrapped entirely around a frosty water glass and peeking nervously out at the restaurant, Molly knows that the date is going to be an incredible success, that it is the beginning of what is called a love connection. She has already determined their couple name: it is Molmeg.

Megan throws herself out of her seat when she sees Molly coming, like a seaman flailing for rescue, and her reaction is so sudden that she bangs her knees on the underside of the table and briefly doubles over with a mysterious squeak of the booth, clattering her elbows on the varnished pseudo-wood. The violence of the attempted greeting is both endearing and terrifying, and Molly feels a surge of guilt (she ought to have announced herself!) and also the frightening desire to laugh. She races forward to the table. "Megan! Are you all right?"

"I'm fine," she says, unsticking her arms from the table. "I'm so excited to see you!" She launches into a hug with

12

the same frantic energy, and she holds onto Molly as if for dear life, rocking slightly back and forth. "Your hair! I love it!"

"Thank you!" Molly replies, unintentionally matching her enthusiasm. (She's been slowly growing it out since the school year ended, because adolescence is a time of changes large and small.)

They huddle up on one tangent of the circular booth-table, and Molly thinks that there is hardly any point to this date at all, that they are already as intimate as they will ever be, as if they've been dating for months, as if they walked in on this story midway through. After dinner, at 6:20, they are going to Cross Pointe to see *Cinderella Man*, starring Russell Crowe, because there is literally nothing else. It is the tail end of June, and the great plains of summer opportunity still stretch endlessly into the horizon.

They both order Diet Cokes and a large pizza to share. The restaurant is still fairly unpopulated because it's not yet truly dinnertime. There is a ridiculous amount of light outside, and Molly occasionally has to shield her eyes from the glare cast by the wall of windows perpendicular to their corner booth. Her double glasses—the soda one steadily emptying, the water one untouched—sweat feverishly. It feels inappropriate for a date. There's another showing at 8:05, but the movie is over two hours long and they both have curfews to keep, Molly's mom is only willing to come out so late to pick them up.

And it is going so well. By Molly's first refill, their hands are already knotted together beneath the table. Megan gets up to pee, and upon her return when she rounds the partition into view, Molly feels herself rise spontaneously in greeting and likewise bangs her knees on the underside of the table, a matching gesture, and she goes down clattering the same way, like they are programmed the same.

When the pizza is delivered, Megan studies it for a while, looking from the pepperoni up to their retreating waiter and back again.

"Which do you think looks more like a ladybug," she asks. "The pizza, or our waiter?"

As Molly ponders this suddenly perfect image—the round, shiny red face of the waiter and his sparkling silver stud earrings, the glistening pizza—realizing this uncanny ability that Megan possesses, that of magical association, she simultaneously witnesses an anomaly: the partition that separates one row of booths from the other blurs in the air and then vanishes like a bad hologram. An ear-splitting roar—like being strapped to the undercarriage of a monster truck while it revs, a monster truck that is also engulfed in explosive fire—erupts around them, vibrating the narrow passages inside her head with a crawling pain, blasting her face with heat. A fiery crater rips wide in the center of the restaurant, expanding like a hole in an old t-shirt when you work your thumbs in and tear it open, splitting the earth along a million tiny seams, devouring everything around their booth. Below the opening stretches an enormous, roaring lake the shade of cooking oil, churning and boiling, frothing with movement. Their corner booth is uniquely positioned at an architectural key point in the restaurant's foundation, meaning that for a second after they leap up, they're just standing there perched on a Tetris-corner span of tile as the upholstered seat back and table slide as

14

one into the abyss, and squinting down at it through the veil of heat, Molly makes out a dense conglomerate of squirming, naked bodies beneath the lake's shimmering surface, filling its every inch, while around the perimeter, soot-black figures scamper head-over-heels, shouldering human skewers that they deposit into the lake with their feet, hands, and teeth, like clearing speared cubes of chicken off a kebab. Steam bursts as each new body hits the surface, a fizzing effect, and the mass has to shift to accommodate it before the body is fully submerged. And still the roar overcomes everything, becomes the only sound she's ever heard, what she was born hearing. Flecks of the lake's evil substance spatter her face, splash burning up onto her jeans, her contacts melt out of her eyes, and as their stubborn patch of the floor dissolves beneath them (Megan's final gesture is that of a mime's scream), Molly realizes that maybe what is scariest of all is how appetizing it smells, how much like pepperoni.

III.

It was basically impossible to transition as a teenager in a place like Dayton, Ohio in 2006; Bennett knew this. Moreover, the name his friend had chosen—Margie—seemed squarely planted in 1940s Midwest farmland, which was a statement in the year of *Borat* and *Clerks II*. At times, Bennett selfishly and crudely thought that their situations should be reversed: it felt confusing that while he, cis, like studied Dead Kennedys lyrics and clung obsessively to every scrap of his barely experienced alt-communal West Coast origins, Margie, trans, pored unironically through the 1954 Centerville High School

15

yearbook to find the black-and-white faces of relatives who'd grown up in the same house that she had. Bennett resents Ohio basically because he's not a native, while Margie seems to have made it her own.

Even Flavors Eatery, where the two now sit, seems to exemplify this dynamic: Bennett likes it because the owners are from San Francisco, his homeland for his four initial years, and Margie likes it because the white sauce they drizzle over each dish makes everything taste like ranch dressing. They have wrested the front corner table that looks out at the parking lot and East Franklin Street, no mean feat during the second lunch period at Centerville (which is two blocks away); the fact that they're here now means that they'll have to wait thirty minutes for their food and will have to cram it in order to get back to school on time, but that is always part of the equation. Windchimes and sun-themed art dangle above them.

The husband-owner brings their two cans of Diet Coke to the table. They put orange slices on the glasses here. As always, Bennett and Margie chat vaguely with him; as always, Bennett asks for "news from the home front," as if he's a soldier away fighting an unjustified war, or as if it's every transplant's desire, not so secretly (just look at this place!) to return to their birthplace. "Did you hear? It's finally sinking!" the co-owner quips. Margie smiles into her soda; Bennett's nostalgia is kind of a joke to her.

The first time they'd come here after Margie started transitioning, sitting at this same table, the wiry wife-owner—who looked to Bennett like the physical man-ifestation of every ill-advised health craze rolled into one, meaning she did not partake in the house sauce—approached their table and began absently massaging Margie's shoulders, and neither Bennett nor Margie knew her or her husband's name and the owners didn't know theirs, but generally it seemed like this was a safe place of sympathetically minded people. Lately, whether it was justified or not—whether Margie needed or wanted it or not—Bennett had been noting such places, had been compiling a list in his head. It will be another solid twenty minutes until their food arrives.

To fill this gap, Bennett shares a theory his mother related to him the day before: "My mom was telling me last night how much better she thought the world would be if every male between fifteen and twenty-five had to take a regular dose of estrogen." He says this without knowing exactly how it will land, whether it's more of a "mom's-so-out-there" anecdote or a "mom's-on-top-of-it" anecdote.

Margie's response gives nothing away. "I love your mother. Do you want my orange?" She hands the slimy fruit slice across the table. "It contaminates the soda," she says.

Bennett slurps the orange and then, over the next several minutes, painstakingly wraps the rind into a cocoon of napkin followed by straw wrapper. The table lays barren between them. After a while Margie asks, "What's up?"

Bennett looks up from the tiny mummy. "Hmm? Nothing."

"You're barely speaking."

"No, that's—just." He waves his hand. "Just empty head, that's all."

"As a matter of fact," she says, "you've been barely

speaking for like the last two months. Since I came out."

The accusation buried in this hits Bennett like a bucket of cold water, and all he can respond with is abject denial, physically shaking it off: "No! That's not it at all, I—" And shades of this. Bennett suddenly feels sick, as if the careful hut he'd been trying to build for them was actually made of glass, and now people are throwing rocks at it. Behind Margie, the husband-owner approaches, surprisingly early, wielding the characteristically cluttered-looking plates piled with innocuous greens, white sauce arrayed across them in cyclonic shapes. But the cyclone is within him!

"You only talk about trans stuff now!" Margie is shouting at him. "That's not all there is! It's not like this has evaporated all the rest of my personality! I'm not a ball bearing!"

As he contemplates this metaphor, struggling to find an appropriate response, one that will not wreck their glass hut but will hold up a shard of it and show that it is a mirror, as Bennett imagines saying this, out of the corner of his eye he sees the floor pop like a blister, and the husband-owner disappears into it. And as Bennett rises instinctively from the table to see what's happened, his face becomes a shocked mask, and Margie's falls in response to his, and he realizes that his every move is a disaster, his every word some poorly planned gamble. The restaurant turns freezing, and Bennett feels his lips crack, his hands seize and age forty years. Great chunks of the floor fall away (the counter and kitchen are already gone) and are whipped into oblivion by the winds that pour from the rending hole in the ground, revealing a furious whiteness underneath them, like a snowblind sky,

18

and finally Margie turns around. The restaurant's teenage diners slip on the icy tiles; they crackle to the floor and are sucked away. As their table begins to skid toward the breaching rift, Bennett reaches out and grabs Margie by the shoulder, pulling her from the chair, which glides on without her, and in the couple of seconds they're successfully standing together at the edge of the void, his fingers on her elbow joint, the restaurant and its people bursting like fragile implements dipped in liquid nitrogen and then smashed with a hammer, Bennett glimpses, below them, through the whipping snow and scalding wind, a solitary, naked figure trudging across an endless plain, doubled over himself against the cold. The figure falls to his knees, the skin of his back breaks in a line down its center, and he blooms like a brilliant red flower on the white before his body is grayed out by the ice, buried under another strata of endless snow. And as his Converse inevitably give way on the frozen floor, Bennett formulates the answer to the question Margie is implicitly asking, that everyone is asking, that they've been asking for years, he shouts it to her through his bleeding lips in the blistering gale that obliterates everything around them, he shouts it so loud that his voice cracks, shatters like ice, and the words become instantly a part of the weather, are swallowed between them like a wave in the ocean, a turn in a wheel, between the girl and the pit at her feet, yawning, yes, with opportunity.

THE HISTORIES

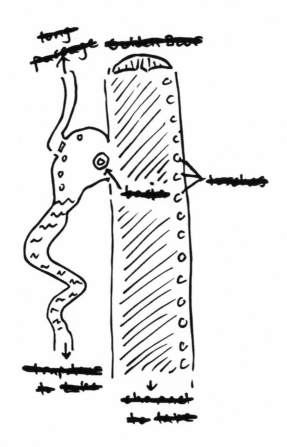

I.

SHE THOUGHT THAT THE moment was probably supposed to be poignant—when she discovered the origins of her name—but since she was sitting on the toilet when she read the letter, it lacked elevation. Henceforth, when she imagined her name, she saw it written out in her father's slanty cursive beneath a harsh yellow light, and behind it, her thighs.

When she finally brought herself to listen to the song—the beat-up 1967 record was among the possessions he'd left her, part of a hoard of cultural memorabilia she figured he'd meant for her "education"—it was, in fact, patterned with words that a daughter might like to hear ("my little darling," "angel," "pretty one," etc.), and carried a message appropriate to a father who'd abandoned his child under dubious pretenses. She could have been singing along by the end of minute two. But only slightly deeper, it revealed itself to be another case of the Conniving Poet, a song about a desperate girl (the eponymous Marianne) and a powerfully disinterested boy, something she could imagine her father listening to while he was wantonly fucking women in 1970s Berlin, a name he'd chosen during the one afternoon he'd assigned himself the task of selecting it, like picking a new insurance policy or rug, scanning his studio on Potsdamer Strasse for relevant influences, his eyes falling on the record, his hand idly down the front of his pants. Visible through the window of the apartment, across the street, there were colonnades, a Jürgensburg horse, but there were no good songs about them.

II.

He told Nikki when she was fifteen, in the first of what was to be her monthly phone call with her father—a smirk she could somehow feel through the phone—and she knew instantly that she hated him. He hadn't told her mother where the name came from those years ago, just left it with her with its appealing diminutive and atypical double consonant and promptly fucked off forever, this stupid little mystery in his wake.

Nikki hadn't known the song or the movie, but as she heard the controversial lyrics for the first time and realized how callous her father had been in telling her now, how plainly vindictive, she felt increasingly like her name had been the first move in a game someone else had set up for her, planted like a goalpost she was only working up to. She didn't like the idea that her $145 Hieronymus Bosch shoes and torn tights were somehow genetically predetermined. She wanted them—needed them—to be singular, and in the aftermath of the call, scuffing alongside the most populated street in her neighborhood, which was mainly a place people came to transfer trains, she imagined the parallel moments: when her father looked down at his newborn daughter and decided that she should be named for the most famous sex fiend in all of popular music, and later, when he felt the stippled holes of the phone's speaker on the corner of his mouth, pictured the body connected to a voice he was hearing for the first time and which, if he played his cards right, he might one day be fortunate enough to meet, and decided that he was ready to relieve this burden.

III.

It happened that we were driving through Ramallah late at night searching for the grave of the poet Mahmoud Darwish. The location of the site was well known to the locals, but not to us, and our driver kept pulling over to ask for directions from passersby on the sidewalk, at traffic lights, on bicycles. He began asking in Arabic, "Where is the grave of Mahmoud Darwish?" But over time, as the night grew later and it became clear that we weren't making any real progress toward our destination, his entreaties became more and more abbreviated and clipped, until we'd reached the point where he would careen toward the sidewalk whenever he spotted a pedestrian, roll down the window, and shout, "*Wen Darwish?*"—*Where is Darwish?*—until the poet became one with his resting place, existed in singular form somewhere between life and death, totemic, connoting all in one a time, a place, and a name.

SECRET MESSAGE

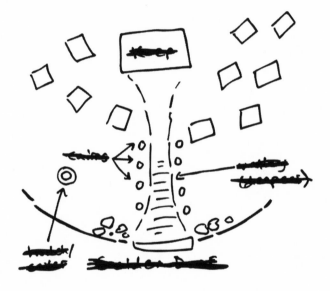

AFTER I TAKE THE secret message from the man at the door, the house becomes rife with codes. In one of the photographs on the refrigerator, I note the conspiratorial way that Rebecca's hand wraps around Henry's shoulder, as if on the verge of absconding. Henry is long-haired and clean-shaven in the photo, the peak of his 60s fixation, Rebecca in her beads and paisley the product. It must have been 2007, the summer after Henry graduated: fascinating, how when you look back on a life that only lasted twenty-eight years, that four-year period doesn't just seem like "college" anymore; it seems like fifteen percent.

Rebecca's lips are pouted for the camera in the manner of a duck, her other hand on her hip. It's startling—unfair—that I remember her name, that this otherwise incidental character, barely a girlfriend, has emerged from obscurity to blot out such a significant portion of this photo, has persisted in making her presence known across these years. I abruptly remember that her scarf came from Kohl's, by my hand. I worry that by putting Rebecca on the fridge, I've unintentionally memorialized her right alongside Henry, alongside everyone else included there, such that the entire surface of the fridge, which is fairly choked with Henry photos—Henry with friends, Henry with family, Henry with culture—is basically populated with ghosts, photographic entities damned by proximity and inadvertently calcified into permanence over time.

I skip across a figure with a topknot and abruptly recall his entire life story—Jared, friend to Henry, and his old-time hippie mother—and all of it feels like stolen ground, like attention I should be sparing for the main event. My mind bloats with the sea of faces, the collage of dead, and I feel briefly like tearing everything down. I tell myself, *Get ahold of yourself, woman. Cool your jets.*

¤

Queen was one of the most popular rock bands of the 1970s and 1980s, routinely playing to stadiums of over one hundred thousand people, and their singer, the late and great Freddie Mercury, is considered one of the most vocally talented and charismatic frontmen of all time. His life was cut tragically short by AIDS. I'm saying this because I'm standing in the eastern corner of the living room, which is where these records are kept, organized chronologically by the date of their recording rather than their release (i.e., *Live at Wembley '86* directly follows 1986's *A Kind of Magic* instead of 1991's *Innuendo*, although the live album wasn't released until 1992, almost six years after it was recorded.) This system is complicated by the fact that the band continued to release albums that incorporated Freddie Mercury's voice up to twenty-five years after he died, like the clothes of a long-gone relative you keep discovering in trunks. As one moves forward in time, the situation becomes increasingly frustrating: Freddie recorded his vocals for "Mother Love" in 1991, for example, the year he died, but the song remained ludicrously unreleased until 1995. So where does one shelve its parent album, *Made in Heaven*? In any event, it isn't long until the foundations of the house thrum with sound, and the answer to the previous question is generally after *Innuendo,* but with reservations.

A watershed moment—no, a pinnacle—in Queen's career came during their twenty-minute performance at Live Aid in 1985, a benefit concert for famished Ethiopia, during which Freddie played conductor to a live Wembley Stadium audience of seventy-two thousand and a broadcast audience of two billion, widely regarded to be one of the Greatest Rock Performances of All Time. Famously, their soundman sneakily cranked up the levels before Queen's set, making them louder than everyone else, louder than hobgoblin Paul McCartney or the Who (who were basically a sputtery series of reunions for old fools by then). Every band that existed in 1985 wishes they were a part of Live Aid.

Our audience was infinitely smaller. We'd lost our son—or I'd lost him while AJ sort of wandered away (name for a father! I should have known)—but that's never been a secret; it's right there in the photos on the fridge, in the bedroom, in the stairway, on the mantle, in the mail that still comes with the yellow forwarding stickers. Still, these days people don't know anything unless you announce it—if you carry around photos of babies, people are going to assume they're yours; by the same token, if someone pries the truth out of you and you answer something like "his brain was eaten," they are not going to take you seriously, even if it's true, they are going to demand a better answer. I waited on a set of instructions that never arrived, a guide to how one made something like this public. I'm still waiting.

Last month, a neighbor lady asked me how my son

was doing, clearly having forgotten his exact name, and I thought, how dare you approach me directly on the suburban street where I live, and I answered that "the industry has metastasized into every man and his laptop," which was a strange verb to use, and she replied that it was a hard climate for sound engineers. And for a second we stood there facing each other on the street, her in her leather jacket and me in whatever I was wearing, perhaps an alma mater sweater, and I thought that we both knew much more than we would ever admit, that we were in on the same dark and unanswerable truth. It *was* a hard climate for sound engineers.

I asked abruptly if she had an ankle tattoo. The way she scratched at the back of her right calf with the opposite foot, I knew the answer before she even opened her mouth.

♮

Freddie Mercury died in his home on the evening of November 24, 1991. The obituaries that followed the next day were universally crass and patterned with money; the tone was very much "gay dragon dies in his castle." Queen's record sales, which had flagged for years, surged morbidly upwards. It's hard to watch a contemporary video like 1991's "These Are the Days of Our Lives" and not to be torn apart by what so obviously seems like imminent death—it was shot in black and white to mask the severity of Freddie's physical deterioration—not to look at him and his cat-print vest with the nostalgic condescension ingrained of our age and think "cute old queer." There are apocryphal stories about how, once Freddie knew his time was limited, he spent as long as he could in the studio, recording material he knew would be used posthumously; anything they wrote those final few months before he took to bed, Freddie sang for them. And of course there was a moment years ago when, touring the control room, Henry showed us an upstart band performing through the glass and then turned a dial on the board, rendering them mute, and I found their earnest silent gestures hilarious, their desperate hands making no sound. And still I'm sitting there on the other side of the glass, the message tucked safely and warmly in my palm, on the verge of spilling everything, struggling to decode their signals, the voice of a golden god wrapping my ears, five full octaves wide, enough for anyone to crawl inside.

PARTNERS

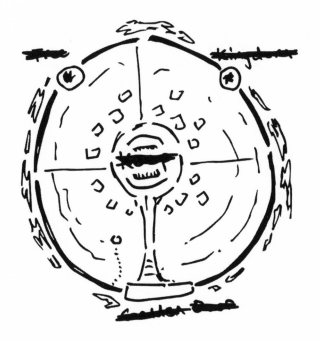

I.

WE'RE IN THE JUNGLE this time.

Here, in this latest environment in our history of running away, the heat mixes rain and sweat.

"It fucking rains all the time here," you say, and I want to kiss you hard until the sun comes out or the rain stops, whichever happens last.

We feel so tiny among the prehistoric plant life.

"I hate the fucking jungle," you say.

The jungle answers you with jungle sounds. You grab my sleeve and hold me tight against your legs, which are pulled to your chest. We are wet and together. The giant leaf we're huddling beneath drips fat rainwater at our feet.

I hug you close even though it's all your fault. Your hair has never been this color before.

I reach into my pocket and offer you the ring.

And you throw it back in my face.

The jungle rains down its vengeance. It may rain for years.

II.

Now we're adrift at sea.

You're lying on your back on our plank. You've stripped down to your underwear. Eyes closed, arms by your sides, your hair a fan, your bare skin burning. You were always too pale to tan.

We're both wasted and thin at this point. We've been drifting for who knows how long.

There's so much space here for things to drop into and disappear forever. Like you've already done with my ring.

The heat is a dry heat.

I cup my hands in the water and sprinkle some on your belly.

You scream and your body crinkles as if kicked. "What the actual *fuck*?!"

"I was just trying to cool you down," I say.

"Well don't just *splash* me. Have some tact. Jesus."

I smile dumbly, and as you straighten back out I kick your clothes off the edge of the raft.

I take my shirt off and lie down next to you. I bunch it up and tuck it under your head for a pillow.

Sharks surround.

III.

It seems absurd, to be trapped inside a volcano. But here we are.

Everything has burned or melted or been thrown away during the crash. We are both naked. The lava lends us a certain glow.

"This place is gonna blow."

Sure enough, the inside of the earth grumbles and shakes. Debris falls around us, but it's just the little stuff. I tell you that, in so many words, not to sweat it.

"Are you kidding? One direct hit could kill either one of us."

I take you by your bony shoulders. We rub our shaved heads together and feel the bristle of each other, and it feels very safe, but we could be having sex.

I open my palm to find the one thing that survived.

You grab my hand, like for comfort. I show you the ring.

You throw it into the lava. "How could you even *think* of that right now?"

The falling debris grows to boulder size and smashes all around us.

IV.

A house in the suburbs is not as safe as we think.

You're at the fridge for a midnight snack, dressed in your pajamas. The light spills out around you. Your hair is just getting long enough that I can grab it between my fingers.

"Is there anything in here besides exotic cheese?"

I nose in about your neck. I kiss your cheek and wrap my arms around your front. "There might be some pita in the freezer."

We won't last long here before we're discovered, but at least there's air conditioning. We seize with every passing set of headlights.

I carry it in my pocket always now, just waiting.

"I'm sick of the chase. This goddamn rat race."

I'm tired of it, too. I'm exhausted.

A loud crack, from outside.

"Honey."

The windows explode. I yank you to the ground, and as glass flies across the kitchen, I dig into my pocket.

Just give me your fucking hand.

MASTERWORKS

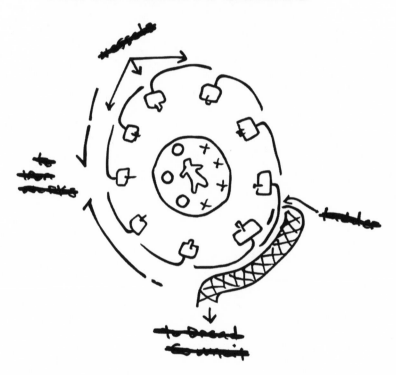

Priam

The Death of Marat
Jacques-Louis David, 1793

THE CURTAIN FALLS ON a terrible summer. Nell finds me lying in the clawfoot bathtub reenacting the famous French Revolution painting of a radical journalist who's just been stabbed to death by an Enemy of the Cause. Her voice comes from above: "Playing dead again, I see."

Startled awake, I jolt upright in the tub, sloshing water over the sides. I try to cover my bobbing junk, because this isn't that kind of portrait—in the original, you only see Jean-Paul Marat's top half (dead), and of course he's all classically rendered muscle where I'm altogether much too hairy—and in the scramble I drop my Booklet of Revolutionary Ideas into the tepid water.

"My treatises!" I cry, fishing it from between my legs, but the ink is already bleeding down the pages like a liberal's heart, the fake blood has washed off my chest, and I can't remember a single poetic thought I've had since I started sitting in here. I throw the sodden notebook across the room.

"How long have you been soaking?" Nell says. "Your skin resembles that of a Gila monster."

"I don't know, a couple of hours."

She scans the candlelit room: it's not the first time I've been caught doing something untoward in the tub. "Speaking of which," she says. "I am in search of my fluorescent lamp. I'm worried the birds of paradise aren't getting enough sunlight."

"I haven't seen your lamp."

There's a dubious pause. The water laps at my knees. In the gap, I try to recall how our last conversation ended: I hear a mis-struck chord on the piano, pounded in rage, and I see Nell's foot disappearing into the stairwell, trailing orange fabric. But the preceding exchange doesn't come, I'm left with just that image—the flash of color, the hateful chord. It felt like days before the echo finally faded into silence, and by then we had acclimated to its tone. That orange cloak—who had we been doing? Tintoretto? Titian?

Before me, Nell is wearing a Frida-like leafy veil over her shoulders, one hand resting on her bare stomach: always posing. She stares down in judgment. "Are you listening to Oasis?"

I am: it's the only incongruous part of my recreation, besides the style of the knife. According to history, after she'd stabbed the newspaperman, the murderess Charlotte Corday didn't even try to escape the house, but waited inside the room to be found, watching her victim bleed out. (In the painting, you can sense her lurking just outside the frame.)

Nell makes an unpleasant face and sniffs the fragrant air; the chiaroscuro created by the candlelight is out of control. "Whatever it is you're doing in here," she says, "keep your fucking paws off my scented candles. And for God's sake, never mix more than two flavors at once."

44

She turns tail and stomps out, letting a beam of hall light harsh my vibe as the door closes. I have to stand and step out of the murky water to reclaim my waterlogged Booklet of Revolutionary Ideas and adjust the mood music, but soon enough I'm back in the tub. I listen to her thumping down the hallway, back to her own solitary projects. Over the past few months it's been reclining tropical nudes via Gauguin and Rousseau, an excuse to pillage the looted department store for expensive furniture and to unearth exotic flora from the overgrown botanical gardens across town. Mine is as good a reason as any to take a very long bath. Lately, it's been these kinds of chamber pieces, elaborate setups that we perform alone.

I slump down in the tub, adjust the towel wrapped around my head, drape my arm dramatically over the edge, and resume playing the martyr. I lean into the music: classic first-album bombast. In my Booklet I write on a damp page, needing to reiterate each letter before it catches, *There is no such thing as property*, knowing full well that everything is just a sloppy excuse for something else. Liam Gallagher swells in my ears—or is it Noel?

We don't belong to each other, I write.

Let go.

Priam

The Garden of Earthly Delights
Hieronymus Bosch, ca. 1500

I'M DOING SOMETHING LEWD with a grape.

Nell creates two enormous papier-mâché blueberries molded on oversized party balloons that we're meant to wear over our heads and stumble around in. There are no eye-holes and absolutely no light gets in.

We don the giant fruit and try to have sex on the kitchen table, but in addition to being blind, I can barely breathe, and I sweat horribly, and our spherical shells knock dumbly against each other, forcing our necks into awkward angles. By the time our relevant naked parts find each other, we're long past feeling amorous. We carry it out with a kind of duty-bound artistic stoicism—hardly a match for the old Flemish master—and when we're both depleted, I rip my fruit head off with a choking whiff of glue and craft-hour, take a great gasping breath, and say something grandiose like, "Eden is dead," but Nell can't hear anything through the papier-mâché. She cocks her blueberry to one side, the paint flaking off where mine kept colliding with it.

Afterward, when both heads are removed, Nell lies on the table while I sensually feed her strawberries from above—indeed the most common fruit in the Bosch painting, though categorically the strawberry is far from luxurious (thematically, a hybrid like a pineberry or nectaplum would make more sense), and it's hard to find much erotic in something that crunches.

She says, chewing, "You should be wearing a bird-like headdress. But I accept this."

It's true: in the Bosch original, humans and wildlife combine in beautiful and unexpected ways, creating an allegorical portrait of appetites unfettered—of paradise found, lost, punished—and there's something spiritually defeating in ours feeling so tame by comparison.

When we've finished, Nell dumps the food scraps in the sink and just leaves them there. She says she's fostering an environment for primitive life to begin anew, as in the first panel, but I suspect it's just laziness.

For the final third of the triptych—dedicated to Hell—Nell digs out a fox skull that is actually probably a raccoon's, leftover from her teenage years as a young pseudo-witch collecting animal bones and uniquely gnarled logs from the woods outside our small Ohio hometown. She mounts it at approximately eye-level, and we do the traditional on the bed, a recorder plugged between us to represent sinful music. Again, it feels like the barest of gestures to the deeply religious Bosch, an afterthought: like, 500 years since he composed his masterpiece, and here we are with the same boring holes.

The next day, in the early morning I return from my ambling to find the building entirely dark. I negotiate my way up to the kitchen on the second floor, and in the orange glow that flickers through the window, I make out a shape at the table.

Suspecting something big, I flick on just the light closest to the doorway, leaving the corners of the room in dramatic shadow. Nell is sitting there, completely still, holding our best woodworking knife—the same knife I'd borrowed to do *The Death of Marat* a month ago. The table has a new rune carved into it, a lumpy circle with a smaller circle within it. The interior circle has been left open in a pained sort of way, the edges not quite meeting. I notice for the first time how many there are—the runes fill one long side of the table, and she's started in on a second row. I wonder for the first time if they have something to do with me, comprise some kind of tally, if

I've been less discreet than I think.

Behind her, through the window, the buildings in the distance are all in flames again. A rotten smell hovers in the smoky air, fruit gone fleshy. My body thrills with authenticity.

"Now," she says, "it's time to talk a little bit about faith."

The word misses me for a second: I hear *fate*, I think *Fate of Man, third panel*. I'm lost to sudden visions of hellscapes, giant ears and eggshell-beasts trampling across the horizon, little demons skating on thin ice, burning houses of worship, miniature chimeras—enough to dodge my place in this.

She's staring at me, waiting for my response. I'm somewhere else entirely, unaware of how much time has passed. The room is filled with invisible smoke.

My eyes prickle and she blurs, the knife blurs, the runes on the table blur. The circle closes.

Nell drops her head to the table.

I blink, and it breaks open again.

Nell

Oedipus and the Sphinx
Gustave Moreau, 1864

PRIAM AND I WERE living at the time in an empty theater in a once-central part of town. Our reproduction involved a stray cat fitted with feathery wings and a har-ness. We named him Peter, after the fact, and like most cats, he was a breaking point.

Beneath the spotlight, Priam, as Oedipus, draped a

patterned tablecloth over his otherwise-naked form in a tasteful way fitting the conventions of nineteenth-century French oils (no bush), I adjusted the pulley system so the hook dangled at just about chest level, and then I retrieved our sphinx. Peter—who often roamed the neighborhood in absence of his people, redolent of the scent of other cats (something like Priam in those days, not that I had noticed it yet)—was lean and feisty and the color of beach sand, but once I latched his harness he went limp, hanging dejectedly in the air like the pendulum of a grandfather clock.

At the mythic crux depicted in the painting—when the sphinx asks Oedipus this quintessential metaphorical riddle about human existence and the ignorant, bloodthirsty motherfucker gets it right—Priam stepped forward, and the cat sprang back to life, fastening his paws to Priam's waxed chest. I saw him wince; to stay faithful to the original, we had to finish before there was blood. In his left hand, Priam held a prop spear, filed sharp.

He fixed upon the cat a steely conqueror's gaze, the look of someone who'd killed his father for not shifting lanes quickly enough, and sensing this—his power or lust, maybe—the cat raised his animal eyes to meet Priam's. I thought, *There, that's it.*

There existed one eerie photo of Priam and I together, taken way back at a party in our vacated past, lit by psychedelic red and green, a photo that has no basis in the history of fine art, but in which our eyes are locked on each other in exactly the manner of the Moreau painting, like we're engaged in some eternal prophetic struggle on a plane beyond this one, or else are completely in love. The picture is long gone, but it always made me wince, less from the raver-kid fashion and bad lighting than because I never knew which of the two it was. I'm even wearing a fucking tiara.

Onstage, something came unhitched and snapped from its tether in the riggings behind us, and suddenly the cat ripped free from Priam's chest and shot straight up into the rafters on its harness with a sound like an enormous zipper endlessly unfastening. We stared in shock as the cat went up and up and up into the darkness. The rope just kept going.

"By the grace of Zeus," Priam said, in this moment very apparently naked. "He can fly." He was bleeding, and the tablecloth pooled around his feet.

Lingering there, beyond the bounds of the painting proper, where Oedipus now stood alone staring blankly up, I took the occasion to propose a riddle of my own: "What's born in a chamber, ages without growing up, and dies without bloodshed?"

The answer was a turtle raised in a terrarium who then died twelve years later, palm-sized, or any number of other things you keep indoors, but I watched Priam's caveman brain turning over itself to try to connect these traits to the cat, to himself, could basically see him repeating *cat, me, cat, me, cat* in his head, silently at first, and then loudly enough to almost drown out the zipper-sound of the pulley, still pulling up, whisking into infinity. But he never got the answer, and, sure enough, the cat never came down.

Priam

Witches' Flight
Francisco Goya, 1798

THE END ARRIVES AS Samhain draws near. Nell locates the photos I have hidden on the computer. "I see you're into group stuff now," she says, the disgust evident in her voice.

I don't have even a glimmer of response; sometimes things just get rude, and the photos are too amateurish to have come from anywhere else. Nell doesn't mention it again, and I spend a quiet forty-eight hours listening to the *Suspiria* soundtrack on repeat and working in my room on my woolly bats and arcane twig constructions; it's harmless spookmeister stuff, not everything needs to be canon. I let the threat of an argument sink and disappear.

Next day, from the rubble of the burned buildings a half mile away I unearth a single human finger. It's a particularly mysterious find: no deaths were reported in the recent spate of fires, and most of the neighborhood has been abandoned for weeks. I keep it in a private place for the right time.

When I return to our building, Nell is sitting in the otherwise-empty ground floor living room with four guys who look like cartoon versions of people you experiment with in college, all arm tattoos, chokers, and dramatic haircuts. She and two others are holding enormous, double-pointed conical hats painted in pastel colors.

"This is Knox, Samsa, Rafael, and Tim," she says, motioning to each in turn. They nod or tip their conical hats. The fourth one just shows his teeth, which have filed points.

"Excuse me," I say, edging off toward the stairs. "I believe I have some latticework to attend to."

"Latticework," says one of the visitors. "What a fruitcake."

Closed in my room, I put on my headphones and try not to dwell on the dark magic probably occurring downstairs. Instead, I turn the volume of the soundtrack way up and focus my attention on the branchwork, twining together pieces of the scavenged forest. There's a delicacy to the art, a careful balance of force and resistance in how much you're able to warp each minute limber twig before it snaps. It represents the shimmering veil separating nature and humankind, our world from the next, ritual from superstition, etc. I've piled the bats into the claw-foot tub on the other end of the room; the branch sculptures are scattered around me.

By the time the soundtrack loops itself, I've created an object of almost heartbreaking tenderness: a five-pointed star made of gnarled branches, a gap at its center like a sightless eye. I remove my headphones to appreciate the beauty of this eminently seasonal object unfettered by the filter of technology, but oddly, the theme to *Suspiria* continues to play. In the same instant that I realize the music is actually coming from elsewhere in the building—that Nell is using the same soundtrack for her own purposes—I intuit a presence behind me. Her voice scares the shit out of me.

"Hey. Crafty McCrafterson."

I whirl around and send various twig sculptures in all directions, except, of course, for the one I grip tightly in

52

my hands. Nell can't help but laugh at my disarray.

"Your presence is requested below deck," she says.

She's wearing the largest conical hat, with matching colored fabric wrapped around her waist. Her belly just dips over the fabric; I think idly that the eighteenth-century palette does not flatter her. The moon throws its crazy light across her in bendy streaks. The sticks do the same on the floor, like fingers reaching out.

The points of the star dig into my palms. The grit gets under my skin, mingling with what's already inside. I'm still crouched on the ground.

Nell shifts her weight impatiently; the top of the hat bobbles. "We require a sacrifice."

I climb to my feet. My human stuff dribbles from my hands to the floor in front of me. The rest of my twig constructions drag it back toward them, a reverse-trickle along the floorboards, their shadows changing just slightly. It dawns on me that, between the two of us, there is no upper limit, that in this moment I'm drawing the extremes of the situation past any ending that isn't dissolution. But that's the movement I'm in, and there's nothing more enthralling than all the elements working together as they're meant to.

Nell swallows, once. I see it travel through her entire body, top to bottom. "Okay, Crowley."

Out of the tenebristic shadows, ever so slowly, we all begin to rise into the air.

Priam

Sarcophagus of Harkhebit
Anonymous, 6th century BC

BAD MAGIC: THE BUILDING shakes once, as if roused from sleep, and then it throws us to the ground. Yells and footsteps come from below. As the reverberations settle, Nell raises her face from the floor, coated canvas-white in the displaced plaster. A dark line of blood runs from her nose, and I know it's over.

I run before she otherwise reacts, before I know how wounded she is, and as I burrow into the crawlspace I tell myself that I'll have to live with this lack of knowledge until it resolves itself, that it's better for me to be hidden and unknowing than exposed and aware. I clatter the grate into place behind me and crawl on hands and knees into the tunnel, close at hand but essentially as far away as humanly possible, until there's room enough to stand, to ease into place among the invisible workings of the building.

I stand very still, the way most inanimate objects do, and my eyes strain to gather the darkness into anything concrete. Dust settles over me. A pipe at my shoulder hisses out a ghostly rhythm. I hear a concerned muffle of voices, a stutter of alarm, the sound of a person being tended, carried, relocated. I hear my own breathing. I wait. I rack my brain for referents, for forgotten antiquities, until it means something more than me, more than just us. *I've let go*, I think.

In time, the others assemble to find me. Inches away from my precious temple, spike heels and combat boots creak across the hallway, a search party combing the depths of the tower where I once lived.

The original lay sideways in a shaft of solid bedrock sixty feet below ground for 2,500 years, stone all the way through, an impossibly heavy object lifted from its underground tomb via a complex system of pulleys and then beached on the desert floor, indelicately emptied, its shriveled, nearly-gelatinous human contents reapportioned to different continents, auctioned to institutional buyers. Still, I wonder if my breath alone could do it, if the residue of my paltry little pulse could moisten these surroundings enough that the rotten beams give way, and I'll go pouring right out. My heartbeat jitters into the hallway.

A layer beyond me, someone uses their knuckles and nails to trace out verses from the Book of the Dead on the walls, describing the passage from one world to the next, testing for structural supports and the gaps between them, listening for an echo or the lack of it, for the evidence of someone stowed away inside. The building was big and rambling, but I hadn't had sense enough to change floors. The vibrations resonate around me, cozying into the exact shape of my body.

"I have an important question for you," Nell had said once, when my body was yet filled with blood, one of my tender limbs held out in front of her, immobilized and primed for the cast. "Are you a shooter or a dribbler?"

I answered immediately, "I'm a quitter," and it was a long, loaded silence that passed before I realized that this wasn't one of the options she'd offered, and so it just hung there between us, innate of nothing, while I tried frantically to turn to stone.

Outside, someone hears an inconsistency, the intake of breath. The verses stop: in the silence, a drawing back.

A human hand decked out in skull rings rends through my plaster tomb, in reality the shitty walls of our third-floor hallway, no good at keeping secrets. After one fumbling second, it finds my arm.

I emit the scream of a lesser being. Bits of plaster pepper the inside of my mouth and begin to congeal. Soon, it coats me from within. The process reverses, inside to out.

I am more mummy than—

Nell

The Dream of the Fisherman's Wife
Hokusai, 1814

THE JAPANESE TITLE OF the nineteenth-century erotic print literally translates to "octopi and shell diver," and the woodcut design is impeccable, each strand of hair, suction cup, and cresting wave meticulously detailed. Its principals—a naked young woman entwined with two hearty octopi—engage in an amorous, onomatopoeia-laden dialogue printed in the background, cramped and ecstatic, the whole work a testament to an era of floating world pleasures and higher lung capacity.

The woodcut's anglicized title—*The Dream of the Fisherman's Wife*—carries the usual patriarchal implications: the husband away at sea, practicing his mysterious and dangerous profession, his wife left alone to satisfy her cravings (insular, provincial, et al) with fantasies about the mythic beasts he brings back tales of. That the sullen and ruminative man she loses for months at a time returns home changed by the depths, her longing and the untold manly horrors he faces in uncharted waters having transformed him into a wild and powerful blah, blah, blah. It's boring substitution. In the original, it's real.

I build the baby octopus first—the mouth-kissing one—as a test of my construction methods. I start by crafting a bulbous plasticine head and then cast a plaster mold around it. I paint in coats of latex, and forty-eight hours later I come out with a rubbery skin that stretches just the way I want. I sculpt a similar mold for the arms, puckering each dainty little sucker with the same TLC I imagine Hokusai applied to his Great Wave.

The daddy octopus takes a full week to build. I gut the couch in Priam's vacant room and wrap the foam around a wire armature, bulking up the head until it's truly massive. I paint enormous half-moon goober eyes on two bowls and jam them into the sockets.

I wrap the first rubberized tentacle around me to ensure it's a good fit. Hokusai knew what he was doing. He sidestepped the tentacle porn fixation that would come two hundred years later and claim his woodcuts as a forerunner. He made it about the mouth.

I spend another day painting in delicate oranges, a few shades away from real flesh. I clear a generous space on the floor in which to spread out. There's more light since Priam left, though it might just be the skyline clearing out. I haven't bothered to address the vaguely human-shaped hole in the third-floor hallway: it's comforting that the most obvious reminder of his vicious departure

57

is so cartoonish, like fucking Wile E. Coyote. The others are long gone, too, obviously; they were only here to populate the painting.

The final piece of the woodcut is easy. I just get naked.

I lie down on my back and navigate the two cephalopods into their positions: the small one by my head, the big one between my legs. I wind the arms around where they should be; they are perfectly flexible. As the original bids, I close my eyes. I imagine bearing forward on the waves. Somewhere near my ear, I pick out a faint whisper going, *Chyu, chyu, chyu.* I dive.

Priam

Doomed
Chris Burden, 1975

ALONE AGAIN, DISTANT, I set a sheet of plate glass of approximately my height against the bare, whitewashed wall at a forty-five degree angle. I set a clock to midnight. I scoot into the triangular opening between the glass and the wall and lie flat on my back. A new home, another sarcophagus. I close my eyes.

It's like one of those structures you make in the woods for the night by draping a tarp over a wayward branch. "A lean-to," I say to myself, momentarily contented with my knowledge of this terminology, as if in another life I might have been a woodsman or a gatherer, someone who uses his hands and wits as a replacement for technology, with full body hair and shapely calves, a tendency toward shirtlessness.

"I was prepared to lie in this position indefinitely," the renowned body artist said later, after the project had ended and he was speaking again. It was an experiment in interference more than anything else: over the span of two days, thousands of spectators passed through the gallery in the Chicago Museum of Contemporary Art, like pilgrims to a shrine, singing songs and throwing their underwear. All the while, Burden laid still beneath the sheet of glass and the ceaseless clock.

In the end, I'd run long past the point at which I was fleeing, and truth be told, I wasn't sure if anyone had actually chased me when I'd run. Still, when I found the building—an old warehouse, in some recent decade a converted performance space—I felt like I'd arrived somewhere. I heaved open the door and looked around as my eyes adjusted, surveying the cavernous space not for how I might be able to cobble together a sustainable existence using its materials, but rather how I could use it as a set. How I could make it into artifice.

The Burden: sparse and perfect.

I lie, and I wait.

I honestly did not consider how annoying the clock would be. I strain my ears to try to pick up instead on curious potential sounds from outside the room—footsteps in the cavernous, barren halls, voices through the garage-like doors on the building's scarred edifice, foot traffic in the desolate streets, explorers—but anything I could possibly hear is overwhelmed, drowned out by the clock.

Forty-five hours into the original, a concerned museum guard placed a pitcher of water near Burden's head, within reach. This was the interference he had been waiting for.

Burden stood up immediately, walked to the next room, and returned with a hammer and an envelope containing his artist's statement. He smashed the clock, stopping time, and opened the envelope. The performance ended.

In another classic display of bystander bait, Burden had lived for three weeks on a platform mounted so high on a gallery wall that no one could see him or confirm that he was actually above, surveying from afar. I'm even more successful: no one knew that I was here to begin with. My breath fogs the tilting glass to one side of my face.

True to form, I've left an envelope in the room next door, explaining everything. It uses words like *audience* and *intent*, excerpts from my Booklet of Revolutionary Ideas. It lists my various apologies.

I have no idea what I'm waiting for. No—of course I do.

Out of nowhere, a human hand plants itself on one side of the glass, right where my breath has made it cloudy. The hand drags across the glass and leaves behind a dewy, ghostly print. My body shivers in the anticipation of movement, of smashing time; I feel unstoppable, like my solitary project has proven a resounding, unqualified success. I hear applause.

The hand draws back inside the glass—it's just my own.

The clock beats on.

Priam

Adagio for Strings
Samuel Barber, 1936

THE CLASSICAL COMPOSITION—widely regarded to be among the saddest ever—was a record we returned to time and time again in our early days, one that had the power to imbue any moment with hilarious grandiosity. We would be caught in some domestic act like breakfast or shitting or stitchery when one of us would sneak the record on, it would suddenly blast out of thin air so loud that it filled the building, and we would be obliged to momentarily freeze, to slowly meet each other's gaze across the room as the strings began their dramatic rise, and then we'd resume whatever we were doing in slow motion as the piece soldiered on, while holding eye contact and slightly trembling, as if this breakfast was the last we were ever to share on earth, or this shit was actually the expurgation of all evil made manifest, or this stitchery was our son's cloak rent from battle, and we knew as the audience knew that no amount of handiwork could ever stitch our family back together again. We were never able to sustain it for long before we broke into hysterics, before we dragged out the props to recreate whatever grotesquely dramatic scene from any of the 144 movies that used this song.

My favorite sequence, of course, came from *Platoon*, when Willem Dafoe, abandoned by his company on the jungle floor, bursts from the trees with swarms of VC at his heels, theatrical explosions decimating the background, gets shot about fifty times in slowmo, and then finally, falling to his knees, reaches his arms up, Christ-like, at the passing helicopters of his squadmates. I always had a bit of a jungle kick and a knack for pyrotechnics, and we used the Gauguin plants as a backdrop, and I dressed as Willem Dafoe and Nell dressed as the Viet Cong and got to wear her ghillie suit, and we rigged the entire second floor with firecrackers. It was breathtaking.

Nell's personal preference was more understated but equally logistically complex: the closing scene in David Lynch's *The Elephant Man*, where disfigured outcast John Merrick lies down on his cot to asphyxiate and die, himself mimicking an eighteenth-century drawing of a sleeping child he has hanging on his wall (a replica of which we had, obviously, hanging on our wall). We spent hours on the prosthetics, layering Nell's face with rubber and plastic until it was physically difficult to hold up, and she spent even longer on the model cathedral Merrick had in his flat in the movie, the way a nervous father obsesses over a dollhouse for his spoiled child.

The tragedy of the movement is almost national: fitting, that its performance has become the go-to catharsis after every televised disaster, the soundtrack to every president's funeral. The orchestral arrangement, the shifting melody and escalating suspense—it is calculated to stop every heart. Most striking is the four-chord climax of the piece, the shrillest moment of crescendo—in *Platoon*, when Sergeant Elias falls, the helicopters soar past (the ground's too hot to go back), and Charlie Sheen grows into a man—which, when I hear it, always makes me imagine standing on a precipice outdoors, like on a cliff or bluff or somewhere remote and windswept where maybe I'm about to pitch myself off, where I dangle my foot out into the salty air above jagged rocks, but for Nell it always summoned the exact moment when, from above, a beam of white light pierces the absolute darkness of a well or cave where she's been sitting for an indeterminate amount of time, her death presumed, and this light signifies hope or the idea of hope, and maybe as the song builds the light gets wider, the gap opens up, and there's someone on the other side of it, a rescuer, and that very contradiction—where one of us chooses death, the other finds life—maybe it ought to have meant something to our paint-splattered selves at the time, in our racist hats and combat medals and suffocating fake noses, should have clued us in on a gulf that we were always skirting, no matter the project (like, I was reenacting suicides while Nell did fresh-faced portraits of youth with fruit accompaniment), such that, however many months later, after our separation, if I was to turn the corner on a dust-covered street within spitting distance of where we once lived, no other humans around at all, and I saw Nell walking toward me from afar, unmistakably, and this fundamentally sad song was somehow filtering through the air and through our heads like the scene in a movie where the army trucks are piping diegetic ennui from their loudspeakers while fallen soldiers are scraped off the beach and all the ladies and gentlemen and children and bandaged brothers-in-arms take off their hats and look to the sky to say, *Yes, this was a tragedy,* and if we were to start running toward each other as the music built again, step by step, our faces opening up in recognition, the world desolate and wrecked around us, when the music reached its pinnacle at the moment of potential reconnection, as our paths drew parallel, maybe it would be in our best interests to just keep running.

Priam

Madonna and Child
Various

I ASKED NELL ONCE if she'd ever considered having children—not because I wanted to have them necessarily, but because there was a silence I was either trying to fill or stretch endlessly into the future. She was standing at the window with her hands on her hips as if surveying her kingdom, and there was something in the dismal, slowly emptying buildings beneath us that reminded me of posterity. It was before they burned, months before I left. I was barefoot, as a pilgrim.

It worked. I'd barely gotten the words out when she broke into a peal of crackly laughter. "Have you ever seen a baby in a medieval fresco? They look like fucking monsters."

"I hadn't noticed."

"You wouldn't. It's not you who has to push one of those lizard creatures out your hooha."

This couldn't be argued, and I was fully prepared to let it go, but a few hours later she motioned me over to where she was perched guru-style on the couch with a book open in her lap. I sat down, honestly thinking we were going to look at old photos—knowing in the back of my mind that we didn't have any surviving photos, yet briefly deceived by this cozy domestic happening and the promise of warm nostalgia—but when Nell turned the book to me, suddenly I was staring at the most fucked-up baby in all of the Western canon. He was a sickly shade of gray, shrunken-headed, and stretched at least twice the length he should be. He lay splayed in his virgin mother's arms, open to the world, an absurd little six-pack doodled onto his stomach. The hairstyle resembled that of a balding forty-year-old. His mouth, fully teethed, opened mid-moan, the eyes half rolled back; he looked to be in utter torment. Dual halos rose behind the heads of mother and child like gilded suns.

"Notice the abnormally long fingers," she said, tracing them with one of her own. Our long lost cat, Peter, felt close to the conversation—hovering on his borrowed wings, maybe—but she didn't mention him. "And look at that tiny. Little. Pecker."

She left me alone to study the book. It was hard to imagine that the fiendish creature aswaddle in red and blue fabric would one day grow into a human-sized savior, or anything touched by the divine. As I flipped through the book and encountered similar compositions on nearly every page, I was struck—as countless others before had been—by the absence of creative material about Jesus' young adulthood: the painters were so obsessed with the extremes of his story (his miraculous birth, his extensive and impermanent death, his apocalyptic return) that they left out the middle. I wanted to follow him through his teenage years and see what was least godly. I imagined roughly the shape of a toddler at my feet, knee-height and blathering. "What a vanilla character," I said.

Nell fluttered back into the room—that's the only way to describe it; her feet barely touched the ground and there was definitely some kind of buzz—and held an enormous Seder plate up behind her head with one hand. It had been stashed in the cupboard since before we arrived. Faintly, encircled around her head, I discerned the printed outlines of the symbolic Passover foods this platter would once have been used to hold: the shankbone, for the yearly sacrifice, the bitter herbs, to represent the lasting tang of enslavement in Egypt. I bobbled a pair of tiny invisible arms in the air. Nell brought her hands out from behind her head, as if in echo, and wiggled them around.

"Who am I?"

The plate hovered there for a second, improbably, saint-like, and then it came crashing down. We feasted on crumbs.

The next day I revisited the book of medieval religious art, but I could no longer locate the ghastly baby. Page after page, in every configuration of virgin, saint, child, angel, and throne, they were the most glamorous and well-proportioned infants I'd ever seen, radiant, their futures robust, full of holy intent and, most especially, character.

Nell sat down beside me and settled into the cushions. "Aren't they beautiful?"

Priam

Magic Scene with Self-Portrait
Pieter van Laer, ca. 1635

OVER TIME IT BECAME increasingly difficult to

qualify our desires outside of the art that we reenacted. Thus, scarcely after we'd mentioned the child, there came the Father.

On that auspicious day, I'd masked my hair with an avocado, olive oil, and lemon juice mixture I'd read about on the internet to give it that extra shine, after letting it grow out for months. Nell appeared in the mirror behind me, leaning against the bathroom doorway and peeling cheap latex monster gloves off her fingers, fresh from the costume store, one of the last businesses downtown to shutter. She stretched one of the rubbery red fingernails out and let it snap back. "I feel like a trick-or-treater."

The self-portrait was minor van Laer, and I'm not sure in retrospect how it came to our attention: the artist recoils before a table appointed with sinister implements and a smoking cauldron, having successfully conjured the devil, whose goofy-looking claw edges in from stage left.

"Pieter van Laer invented the concept of the monster glove before anyone else had even fathomed the technology," I said. "He was a revolutionary."

"More like a Rosemary." Nell took in the sight of me luxuriously dragging a comb through my wavy locks, smooth as butter, while simultaneously contorting my face into grimaces of terror. "Your head smells like a bowl of guacamole."

At length, we moved to the gloomy tableau we'd set up downstairs, its vessels and vials arranged (with an almost floral panache) to suggest the height of spookiness, an aesthetic to which Nell was wholly opposed. The occultism of the Dutch-born van Laer's low-genre scene, with its array of conspicuous and predictable arcana, wasn't fine-tuned enough for her tastes, nor as sophisticated as that of his Golden Age contemporaries.

Nell flipped through the various Evil Tomes I'd assembled in the way you'd look at the art projects of someone else's child: mildly appreciative of the effort and muscle control it took to create them, but plainly unimpressed. "This isn't even competent hexery," she said, dangling the most prominent volume by its delicate cover (which I'd wetted and then dried by the furnace to give that weathered look). "Look at these drawings. A pentagram? A heart with a knife in it? This is some hokey fourth-grade shit."

She ripped out the illustrated folio with a savage enthusiasm and cast the pages across the room like heretics from the altar, then brought out a new sheaf and set to work on their replacement.

Her brush hand, now gloveless, moved in quick, precise motions while the other rotated the page beneath it at intervals. I wanted to tell her that it was about integrity rather than strict faithfulness, especially where the Devil was concerned—like, just because late Matisse figures were basically emphatic crotchless scribbles didn't mean we could scientifically reduce our bodies to a couple of fluidly connected knobs and hack off our you-know-whats—but I stayed quiet; I lit a thick candle and watched it steadily burn down, guiding the wax dripoff with my fingers.

Occasionally, I'd steal a glance at Nell's progress across the room. Her concentration was beyond intense, and above her wrists nothing seemed to move. For a moment, I thought I saw a third hand, barely visible, operating among the rest.

She finally stood, knees cracking, and opened the book

to me, her new pages stitched in. "Is that not the sickest little fuck you've ever seen? Does that not look blood-swelled and ready to burst?"

I examined the book in the flickering candlelight. There were a dozen or so images drawn across two pages, tracing the development of some slit-eyed, vaguely humanoid creature with mottled pink flesh and an over-sized, veiny head; I could barely stand to look at it. I studied the text below each illustration. Twelve weeks, fifteen. The vocabulary was beyond me. "I didn't know you spoke Latin," I said.

"I don't speak Latin. Are we set here?"

"Almost." I set the skull to smoking, adding a little of this and that. When I looked up, I caught Nell silently mouthing the words freshly inscribed into the book.

Palms sweating, I examined the diabolical canon on the scroll of parchment elsewhere on the table before me, as if to verify its melody. I turned away from Nell and the book in the pretext of finding better light, tracing that crucial verse: *Il diavolo no burla* . . . Out of superstition, I changed a single note.

I turned around again while tossing my hair back—it was a gesture I'd affected since growing it out—and it caught on the embers of the hanging lantern, sizzling slightly. I ducked and frantically fanned the ends.

"Aw, *Bamboccio*," Nell said, her voice dipping into the register reserved for those either gravely wounded or recently born. She lovingly twirled one side of my mus-tache (which had taken weeks to root) and laid the book back into place among the other grimoires. Her hands flickered out of the frame. Beside me, the inverted skull smoldered in anticipation, as did the tips of my scented

69

hair. The air in the room went slowly from Taco Tuesday to Human Barbeque.

I smoothed the amended canon out on the table in front of me and let out the most delicate of breaths. Suddenly it all seemed too real. Nell put her hand over mine. Her fingernails were longer than I remembered.

Weeks later, when I was finally clearing off the table, I found the first rune carved into one corner: a crude star, like you'd find done on a tree trunk by a thirteen-year-old or, truth be told, in one of van Laer's spellbooks. I couldn't tell how long ago it had been carved. Over time, as the collection of carvings spread across the tabletop, the technique became more accomplished, as did my studious denial of it. But it took forever to match the two, and by the time I did, it was too late.

Nell

St. Francis in the Desert
Giovanni Bellini, ca. 1476

MONTHS GONE, I'M POKING around the very fringes of the ruined city long past smoldering, far from Priam, when another wave of morninsg sickness hits. I plant my hands on my thighs like a running back braced for impact and sort of teeter there, rocking back and forth, but nothing comes. The sun cracks over the rocky horizon. My insides swarm and then settle, as if after a tidal wave that forced the evacuation of a coastal fishing village but never made landfall.

I've grown accustomed to my witchy existence out

here since Priam's departure and the crumbling of our home of years, when I could no longer stand the gray city on my own, the enormity of that empty building brimming with stuff. My days are spent in quiet communion with the land, in study (Starhawk, Milton, spellbooks I dragged out in a busted shopping cart), finding harmonic patterns in light cast through the spired projections of distant buildings and the interplay of shadow and scraggly tree branch, offering silent sermons to the birds. There's a makeshift rubble cave that I snuggle into at night, not because I have to.

I stretch myself at its mouth, my stomach still unsteady, for the first time unsure of the habitat I've been building in the months since Priam split, if it's even the least bit sustainable, if I've come too far along to go back. I feel both utterly powerless and as if an enormous responsibility—as big as the city to the east, as big as God—has been foisted upon me, like a cancer or a spiritual calling. It sucks.

It's hard to say whether the St. Francis of Bellini's painting is even a true hermit at the moment of stigmata depicted—the Tuscan-ish city in the backdrop is hardly more than a ten-minute stroll away, and the shepherd looks up from his sheep at the supposed miracle with the kind of nonchalance that implies this kind of thing happens fairly often, more weird neighbor (read: casual witch) than devout ascetic. Like, maybe once a week the not-yet saint slouched back to the city to have his garment carefully pressed. Maybe he enjoyed the folksy grandeur of the Third Order, the reputation that preceded him.

As if in response to this blasphemous thought, my

71

stomach seizes again and the wind kicks up viciously, throwing open one of my leather-bound volumes. The pages flip by and in the unearthly gust settle on a two-page spread that is familiar to me, one of those old multifaceted symbols I've become very good at drawing. I remember hacking a primitive version of it into the surface of the kitchen table after another night when Priam hadn't come home and I'd had something to tell him, a reminiscent kick of betrayal in my stomach.

I had left so many signs. There was evidence everywhere, across every era, mothers and their immaculate and horrendous children. What was our chock-full building itself but a rambly-ass metaphor for reproduction? He must have known that I was counting weeks. He must have seen me growing. He must have.

I'm suddenly standing again, the book at my feet, my arms spread to either side, palms out. A beautiful, terrible light bears down from above. The wind is furious, and a lone feathered tree bends toward me beneath a great and invisible weight, but my robes remain perfectly still. The nausea returns stronger than ever, yet I'm rooted in place, my body a conduit, channeled through like a rod.

On an outcropping near me, a sandy-colored cat looks on in idle curiosity—like the donkey of Bellini's original, a traditional symbol of ignorance, dumbass. *Peter*, I think. *Meet me at the gates, show me where you've been hiding.*

My palms begin to burn, and then bubble. The cat yawns or stretches its jaw. I match his expression.

Years dormant, the sensory memory of being inside a cheap Mexican restaurant vividly overtakes me. We were younger, too young, the walls garish red and the air dense with grease; Priam had cleaned out a basket of tortilla chips and his hands were slick with it, his face was glowing. He pointed to a floral skull painted onto our booth and said, "At our wedding we are going to have a skeletonman who plays dirges on the organ, and our son shall learn the flute," and the commitment implied by this sentence carried almost a threat, and then he received a piping stone bowl with shrimp dangled around the perimeter like the fingers of a massive shattered hand, and I knew he intended something permanent: if I agreed, it would overwrite everything that had passed between us.

I feel the stirrings of another within me. My body radiates at five points. The flailing tree whispers a name I don't recognize, and the city rebuilds itself in the background in splendid array: a sacrament. My insides rise and fall.

At long last I buckle forward, releasing my guts onto my feet and the sun-dappled earth, the land redolent of ash and meat. Peter turns away. He was named for the demon, not the saint.

I remove my shoes in the presence of the holy.

Priam

Messiah
George Frideric Handel, 1741

THE *MESSIAH* WAS SOMETHING we'd done as far back as we could remember. Separately, our parents had taken each of us to an annual performance of the eighteenth-century oratorio by the local philharmonic, until we rebelled (Nell at eleven; me at fourteen) and the tradition withered. I'd speculated that, years back, we may have even attended the same performance by coincidence, and Nell asked if I remembered the year when, during the Hallelujah chorus, the first-chair violinist had stood up and hurled her bow javelin-style through the chest of the conductor, who fell resplendently back into the arms of the standing audience. I said that I hadn't seen that one.

"Well," she said, "I guess that means we probably didn't overlap."

♮

The timeline does not work in my favor any way you slice it, no matter when I finally put the pieces together: Nell was pregnant, and I ran for the hills.

When I do find her again, fully five months after leaving, it's at the mouth of a cave two miles outside of town. Peter led me there: something drew me back to our old neighborhood, and I found him prowling the street across from our abandoned building like a Lazarus back from heaven, a spirit guide. When he fled from me, I followed. He was the first sign of life I had seen for weeks, and so my instinct was to give him everything. He didn't lead me astray.

I find Nell buried beneath a strata of six blankets with a spellbook open on the ground by her feet, resembling nothing so much as an obdurate boulder in a river, the scrubland parting around her, and the baby imminent. As she slumps the blankets off her shoulders, revealing her scrawny frame beneath, her swollen belly, the whole of history comes crashing down around my ears. My mind goes blank: I rewind desperately, trying to remember how I've filled the time since I left, my months of important work in the warehouse, my conceptual experiments, the strides I'd made in creating paint without water, my full beard. But I can remember none of it. All I'm able to summon is the image of an empty chair on white, the presence of an absence: I wasn't there. I was nowhere. In all this time, we'd never been more than five miles apart.

She greets Peter first, but by the name of one of the elder gods. There are no words for me, and besides, I had never deserved them.

We hightail it back toward civilization. The rickety shopping cart serves as Nell's chariot, and I the traitorous beast who pulls it.

¤

The libretto to *Messiah*—compiled from scripture by Charles Jennens and then passed to his longtime collaborator, Handel—has never particularly impressed us. It reads too much like King James' Greatest Hits, as if Chuck Jennens (who famously believed that Handel's composition did not live up to its source material) had spent a summer afternoon in 1741 dipping into the KJB for his favorite bits, the annotative work of a lazy high schooler highlighting the obvious plot points so he has something to reference when called upon in class. In our versions, we swapped out the Bible for quotes from Thelemic blessings, Lovecraft, and Milton's Prince of Darkness, the ancient and the far-below.

¤

We have to take a train to another city to get to a working hospital. Peter abandons us with a howl when he sees the headlights approaching on the platform, probably with flashbacks to spotlights and theatre rigging. Neither of us gives chase—he was always an outdoor cat at heart—and thus our guide departs. Once we're aboard, the movement of the train feels wildly out of control, hurtling to a stop at every station, like its every journey is some terrible gamble. I hold fast to Nell like an anchor, everything newly strange. The landscape goes from desolate to swarming.

The sight of populated civilization after all these months seems unreal, and the hospital-land reads like an alien environment, so bright and relentlessly lit as to preclude the possibility of true sterility. I imagine some poor janitor scrubbing repeatedly at the same corner, failing and failing to achieve Hospital White. It occurs to me as we navigate the hallways that painting is an inherently filthy medium, that it is basically smearing layers of shit made from mashed plant and animal matter onto a once-blank surface. I realize I've forgotten what fluorescence looks like at full strength.

Somehow we get Nell to a bed without having to reveal our names, and suddenly I'm standing alone in a grand hallway symmetrically aligned with hateful flower artwork and flanked by an empty waiting room, watching the doors of fake-looking varnished wood swing silently forward and backward on well-oiled hinges as uniformed personnel scurry in and out. And then I'm racing after her again.

¤

Hours later, a child is born into a sea of beckoning gloves on a bed I'm convinced will never be clean again. When he emerges fully into the room, hospital staff frantic around us, the tone I hear—the musical association the baby inspires—reminds me of one of Handel's most ethereal moments in *Messiah*, the chorus in Part III stipulating that resurrection comes as easy as death, where the younger the kiddie choir that sings it, the more haunting it sounds. I envision a sky in roiling flame, unearthly but strangely peaceful. When I put my index finger out and his little baby hand can't even throttle it, I feel gargantuan, god-like, and in the realization of our totally disproportionate sizes a wave of tenderness washes over me, a sheltering instinct, and I know that he is mine, in some way, but also that he fundamentally isn't.

¤

What seems like seconds after the room is cleared, our sweat still drying, the nurse returns and asks if we're planning to stay the night. I look from her to where Nell lies propped on the bed, swallowed by the paper-thin gown, her eyes barely open. I tell her that yes, we will be staying the night.

Nell drifts back off immediately, barely disturbed. The nurse takes her leave. I turn off the lights in the room and sit in the chair by the window, looking out over the strange city below, trailing into the night, its constellation of mechanical lights. Beyond their perimeter, the world pools like a black sea around an island. Within the depths of that sea, I have no idea where we came from.

I feel each minute pass, each adjustment of capital

charging us for the time we spend here, for the space and the services of its people. In another room, the baby grows at an incredible rate.

The next morning, I stand at the counter, Nell beside me in the mandated wheelchair with the baby in her lap, and the receptionist on duty tells me to see the financial counselor. I follow her directions to an office down the hall, heart rising into my throat, the same sensation as being hopelessly, irrecoverably late to an important meeting. I wonder why I haven't started running.

He quotes our bill in a concerned voice, and I lean forward onto his desk, as if to block Nell from the shady dealings, though I left her back at the nurse's station. When I reach into my pocket, I feel sweat run down my side. I draw the card from my tattered wallet, and it's accepted and swiped for thousands of dollars without ceremony. I don't speak at all until the exchange has been entirely performed. I sign my name and return to the station. Nell doesn't acknowledge that anything has occurred.

An electronic pulse echoes out from the hospital terminal and lands on a computer screen somewhere in the distant Midwest, where a man who once took his child to yearly performances of Handel's *Messiah* sits reading in his office. He notes the charge to his account. He is quicker to put the timeline together than I ever was. A son is born, and reborn. *And the government shall be upon his shoulder.*

We emerge from the hospital into the light of day. We called him Morning.

Liam

Fall of Phaeton
Sebastiano Ricci, ca. 1703

THE DOOMED FLIGHT HAS been rendered many times, and ultimately all of mythology comes to rest on the fact that the child always forsakes the parent, one way or another.

The last time I remember you in the house, Priam, after your first year of college, I passed through a room that you were occupying and found its furniture decorated with others, helpless in summer glow. When I asked for introductions, you gestured lazily to your friends en masse and said, "These are my fellow outcasts," like this was a life I'd expelled you from, a dead thing you only returned to for spoils, and I was reminded that your record of history was not to be trusted. It was hardly the first time you'd tried to mask me over, and I coped with the moment, the word, as I had with many others, by picturing its physical bounds: I imagined the facsimile of another son ghosted in wax, slurried and then fired in a kiln and filled with hot metal, which once cooled I'd hammer away, leaving the full figure behind, literally "cast out," yes, this was what he'd meant, exactly as I had formed him, filed down sprues and all, no sign of the mold left on him.

¤

The story goes that mortal Phaeton, upon meeting his father, Helios, for the first time and being granted any wish, asked only to once drive his father's chariot pulled by its legendary flaming horses, which the sun god daily rode across the sky, shedding light on the earth. Here the father waffled—it was folly, Phaeton would not be able to control the horses, the heavens moved swiftly and it was too difficult a course—but the son insisted, and Helios buckled under his promise: he showed him to the golden chariot, he handed him the reins.

And it was inevitable, fated. Phaeton careened through the sky, not knowing the way. The horses ran wild. He veered too close to the earth and set it aflame; he cast his smoke-stung eyes frantically to the western horizon he knew he would never reach; in his panic, he dropped the reins. High above, knowing the earth would be destroyed if he didn't intervene, Zeus, king of all gods, struck Phaeton dead with one of his famous thunderbolts. He fell. The story ends with poplar trees on a riverbank, a metamorphosis of grief.

Ricci's version is finely neoclassical, depicting the moment of the fall absent the spectral effects that characterize other interpretations, the Titians and Rubens and Moreaus. Plunging Phaeton and his father's wrenching horses are front and center (neither aflame), dramatically shadowed, all rippled muscle and artful nudity, while Zeus is wraith-like and out of focus, atmospheric destruction branching from his hands. (In Ovid's text, the light of the blazing horses, the fiery earth, the splendiferous chariot glares out all shadow; a proper interpretation would be cast as beneath the mortician's lamp.)

Ricci renders the scene as simple human tragedy—beautiful human tragedy—a boy far out of his depth, the terrible real. Mine: he cannot be trusted to follow the wheeltracks I've deep inscribed into these roads, this path I have carved for us to travel together. And I recall a much earlier time when we were thus arrayed on our way to school, with me at the helm and you breaking eleven in the seat beside me, suddenly after all these years gone squirmy, early light pinking around us, and when we came to pause at the stoplight dividing one field from the next, you threw open the door and fled into the teeming grains, which swallowed you like an ocean. When I looked out and could no longer see you, son of mine, I can tell you it was like all the invisible titanic stars had come crashing down around my ears, and I knew that I would burn every field in the world if I had to, until you were plain before me. I followed like a harvester follows, stripping the land bare. By the time we returned to the car together, the sun had already finished going up; it'd got there on its own.

A dozen years later, I didn't even know it when you left, you had drawn our distance so wide by then. I was in the workshop and I was fashioning a new arm for one of the chandeliers, North Annex B, I was using a pair of pliers to glob the hot stem, and I noticed the fine red strands pulling within the glass like bloodveins, and this, I take it, was the moment that you, somewhere distant and adult, crossed finally out of sight.

Still, I have always kept a seat beside me for you, and when the transactional notice came from the hospital at St. Mary's—blessed parent—I knew it was a call for help, a sign that the horses were out of control, that they didn't recognize your weight in the chariot, your right to these skies. I knew from this gesture alone where you had gone, who with—I remembered the haircut, a leg flung over one of the divans in my living room, a conspiratorial look—and what must be now that hadn't been before. I felt our dynasty expanding.

I loosened the reins; I permitted the charge to the magic card (as everything in our house was possessed of a magic, the magic of my backing), and I packed what I needed to make it to the shattered East. I have it in my heart, here: unlike the god who traveled the flaming skies of antiquity, I will be there to catch him when he falls.

Nell

Christ Stilleth the Tempest
John Martin, 1852

OUR FEEBLE PROTECTIVE SPELLS go haywire. The rain comes. And comes. Dogs and cats slap down into the streets below and bury them to the first-story windows. We move to the upper floors. It's strange to be back in the building where so much happened, where so much ended, like returning to a childhood home still stocked with your old possessions, each of them charged with emotional memory, unexpected resonance: I had no thought for it while I was elsewhere, but the proximity reattaches me. I rescue what I can—I carry the remains of the plants up the stairs, boxes of books and supplies, the smaller canvases—but there's too much of it; there's not enough room for the stuff and the three of us.

Our first fabrication when we arrived was a sparse crib for Morning: I rigged a little mobile of things—wax fruit, gaudy fake brooches—and hung it above him. It whirled and whipped in the wind; it was always in motion. I thought that this child would know nothing but rain.

As the days pass and the water rises, Priam begins to build a raft. He revisits his old room and comes back with the battered-down skeleton of the couch. He lines the base with empty trash bottles and plastic bags, things that theoretically float. He wags a pair of massive foam tentacles in my face, the delicately applied paint already flaking off. "What were you doing with these? You've savaged my couch."

I crane my head out the window. The water has risen to the seventh floor, just below us. The surface churns and shifts, riotously loud, like a witch's cauldron, and every so often I discern an object beneath it, washed out of another building or picked up off the street to join the liquid mass of the world underwater, briefly suspending itself before sinking. With each level the water rises, it feels like another layer of our past in this place is erased and buried; we become fresher than before, one step closer to being completely new. I ask what Priam thinks happened to Peter, and he makes a bubbling sound with his mouth that seems to please the baby. I pretend Priam did it for him.

"You know what this reminds me of?" I ask. The sky, a bruised gray underlit by flashes of lightning, throws down rain in sheets like the steadily moving spray of a carwash. Thunder rolls up and rattles the windowpanes.

Priam is lashing the largest tentacle around one corner of the raft, like a bumper. There are ways that he has been good. There are spaces I wouldn't have filled on my own. "What?"

"Pollock's *Full Fathom Five*."

He joins me at the window and looks down. There's

a glimmer of pink in the roiling waters; an eye-shape surfaces and then disappears—my octobaby. "Not blue enough," he says. "This is more of a Turner seascape, a hundred years after he painted it." He pauses. "You know, from the decay of the pigments."

"I got it."

A silence falls, and I hear Priam inhale. For a second, I imagine him apologizing. Instead, his voice booms out:

Full fathom five thy father lies;
Of his bones are coral made;
Those are pearls that were his eyes:
Nothing of him that doth fade,
But doth suffer a sea-change
Into something rich and strange.
Sea-nymphs hourly ring his knell: Ding-dong.
Hark! now I hear them—Ding-dong, bell.

He nudges me at *knell*. I leave him at the window. I nurse Morning on the other end of the room, the mobile spinning madly beyond us. Water licks at the penultimate step in the stairwell. I notice that Priam has ridged the long sides of the raft with a line of his twig sculptures, like a sinister decorative guardrail.

I wonder why we came back here when all was said and done, why we couldn't abandon this place as we'd done so many others. We had paused on the curb outside the hospital for a moment, in the sun, and our future had been unclear. I'd stood up from my wheelchair, Morning in my arms. I had the thought that it was only his little hospital-provided hat and onesie that shielded him from the outside world, that somehow kept him from totally being my responsibility, and that the moment this outfit was gone or sullied, he would be open to everything, intensely vulnerable. I resolved to keep it perfectly clean.

In any case, a cloud had slipped, and a light rain started falling, and impulsively we had walked right, toward the train station again, because that path was familiar to us, and there was some saying about magic being rooted to location, and because we had summoned someone into the world and didn't know what to do with him. So we did the same thing we had always done, we returned to a place that had seemed a proving ground for something, and we tried to prove it. But the rain fell harder than we'd expected; it came from beyond to flush us out.

¤

Onto the back half of the raft I load a wooden tray of mason jars half-filled with dirt, my seedlings, a hardbound copy of the collected Blake, a backpack of Victorian-looking clothes. I wrap a layer of plastic tightly over it. Across the room, leaning against the wall, there's a framed reproduction of Thomas Eakins's *Arcadia* that we've carted from place to place since we started moving. I painted it before we knew each other, in the same way that Eakins did with his magic lantern in 1883: I took a photo of the painting and projected that photo onto another canvas, from which I traced it. The layers of filtration from the original—my imperfect photograph, the dilution of the magnifying light from the projector, my skill at tracing, at color matching—pulls it a step further from mimesis, blurs the sharpness of Eakins's oils, the reality the painting depicts. I don't remember why I chose to copy it

85

originally. I've always found something off-putting about the painting, a kind of voyeurism in his naked adolescent models in their would-be paradise—there comes a very real moment in the process when you're detailing a little boy's crotch. I've never believed in the innocence of children as old as the ones in *Arcadia* are supposed to be, or I don't trust the forty-year-old artist's motives in representing it (one of the models became, eventually, his wife). And of course I know why we came back: I look to the raft overburdened with our accumulated junk, its every supplemental feature like something we were trying sheepishly to save, to trick ourselves into rescuing. It couldn't float in a hundred years. It was never enough for us.

I go to the window again; I reach down and skim my fingers over the surface of the water. The sky turns in on itself: spirals of distant sunlight wrap through the swirling clouds, and further out, the remaining patches of the city rise like beleaguered islands, shining wetly in the storm, already ruins. The waves seem to move in every direction, bashing against each other, cresting and falling constantly, bearing up higher than our window. The glassy, vacant eyes of our building peek out just above the surface, on the verge of going under.

And then, on the horizon, I see a distant craft approaching, a point of clarity in the swarming grays. It slowly takes definite form, riding the waves in long arcs forward, navigating the sea haphazardly like a wind-blown piece of origami: a ship.

"Is that—"

"Oh, God."

It rocks terribly back and forth. The golden prow dips

and sprays a plume of water; the sail bulges and ripples, swaying treacherously in the wind. Even through
the storm, or enhanced by the storm, the ship asserts its
magnificence—the complicated-looking riggings, the
dark figures mounted on either side, all designed to be
seen—it's absurd, unearthly. Morning rotates himself
in my arms, ashamed by the opulence; he turns to my
chest from the embattled sea. In the distance, a titanic
wave draws up as if pulled by a hand, revealing the tiered,
streaming city beneath, like a vision from another plane.

"John Fucking Martin."

It takes a moment for the reference to click, but when
it does, the image of Martin's famous version of Jesus on
the Sea of Galilee freezes in my head: the shining ship
in the lap of a terrible storm, the sun breaking through,
the visionary city in the background. There's a pulse of
inscrutable emotion—a moment of beauty and certainty,
of *rightness*—along with a physical sensation, something
parallel to leaping over a chasm and feeling both feet
land solidly on the other side, a breathtaking second of
bodily safety, relief. In the blink of an eye it's gone, com-
partmentalized into the memory of the painting, such
that I'm already winding down and catching my breath
even as the boat continues to rock its way towards us,
rising and diving as if each second will be its last above
water; the significance of the vision has already spiked
and passed. We stand at the window and watch, vaguely
apart. The gigantic wave slams back over the distant city,
swallowing it again. The sky makes a sound like fabric
being ripped.

At the last moment before colliding with the top level
of our tower, the boat veers wildly to the right, swerving

one of its broad decks to greet our window. An anchor falls, and a massive wave spills over the sill, washing over our feet. The raft beside us shifts; its plastic crackles.

Up close, it's clear that the boat, like ours, is a composite of other materials: each varnished slat of the hull is a slightly different shade of brown, and the billowing sail is a patchwork of cloth. Still, the prow and deck are decorated with sculptures painted in burnished gold, mermaids and serpents that share a hand, a certain gothic tackiness, like the builder couldn't help showing off, even on this haphazard, functional thing. The captain steps down from his promontory, which includes a throne, and comes to stand on the deck across from us, the boat rocking beneath his feet. He wears a sopping blue robe, his long, wet hair is pulled back, and a white beard explodes over the lower half of his face. The rains seem to dwindle in his honor.

I look from his narrowed eyes beneath the wild eyebrows—staring at us as if disappointed in the lack of others, as if he'd expected a screaming throng to greet his vessel and fall at his feet—to Priam, standing motionless beside me, his knuckles gone white on the windowsill. For a second, the baby is the only person who moves; he yawns and stretches his arms. As I draw the connection between the two of them, between this man and the shabby wealth of this ship, Priam and his history, I realize the stuff that Priam had always been made of, that he had been fighting and denying and drowning in since we met: it was fear, and it was money.

"Dad," Priam says.

"Father," he replies.

Nell

The Raft of the Medusa
Théodore Géricault, 1819

"PLEASE," HIS FATHER SAYS once we're aboard, wrapping my hand over his. "Call me Hugh. Or, hey, call me Captain de Chaumareys." When I withdraw, the palm of my left hand is indented with the shapes of his rings: a hexagon with a diamond within it, an egg, and a skull. The surname—not Priam's—rattles around my head but doesn't strike anything.

The final floor of the building behind us is finally consumed by the storm. The boat rises with it. In time, the remaining islands vanish, too. The world flattens. In the end, we took nothing but ourselves with us.

I call him Hugh.

Our space on the boat is a ten-foot compartment below deck, opposite Priam's father's post and the captain's quarters on the other end. The room is sized for stowaways, and I sense that there are levels below us eating up the rest of the space, hidden chambers we don't have access to. Within, there's a straw-stuffed twin mattress and a bassinet for Morning that's been crafted with obvious care—the same attention I saw Priam bring to his twig constructions, the branches tied tight and intricate—but inside the bassinet it's spiny and unfinished; the sharp ends of all the little shoots poke into the basket like a child-sized iron maiden. There's an element of dangerous absentmindedness to the bassinet, to its superficiality, the idea of the thing over the use of the thing itself. I insulate it with three layers of thick, scratchy blankets before I introduce Morning to it.

Priam is immediately cowed and deferential in the presence of his father, prone to small and technical arguments. I don't know what this new step means, what we agreed to by coming aboard, nor where Priam's father intends to take us. I get no answers, and I suspect it's because Priam doesn't have them. The storm continues on and off; there are calm periods where it only rains, when the clouds relent enough to push out the horizon and reveal the endless breadth of the waters, that with each hour we likely grow more and more remote.

At times, I peer over the deck railing (properly more of a carved banister) and watch the cities pass below us; ghosted in the waters I see the tops of buildings swallowed by the rain, arrayed at different depths like mismatched stairs leading up, down, across to nowhere, into drowned cities of myth—Ys, Atlantis, R'lyeh—the civilizations said to exist when the unexplored half of the globe was believed to be only water. But there ended up being land there, and then cities.

During one of the stormy periods I visit Priam's father on his perch, where he remains, always, spinning the pegged wheel this way and that. I'm not convinced that it's connected to a rudder. I wave to summon his attention. He lifts his chin at my presence. "Hugh, are there other cities left?"

He pretends not to hear me over the wind and rain. He shakes his head once—*come again?*—and before I can repeat it, he motions expansively before him, his eyes looking through me. "You know," he shouts, "I can't remember for the life of me if it was Turner or Vernet who tied himself to the mast of a ship during a thunderstorm so he could capture the full sensory experience in his paintings. Of course, Victorians in their way were more tolerant of these eccentricities. They respected painters more than we do nowadays." The word "eccentricities" is ripped apart by the wind—it sounds like *ex-en-tis*—but I reconstitute it, I have no doubt of the word.

"Where are you taking us?"

"I've said it a thousand times," he says, though he hasn't told us once, not to my knowledge. The boat rocks to the left, and I brace myself against the arm of his throne. I try to remember where Priam is, if I can trust him to steady Morning in the cabin, to pick him up and calm him. "There's nothing for you to worry about. I'm steering us home." He offers a cursory rightward twirl of the wheel.

"Where exactly is that? Ohio?"

"There are a lot of names for it," he says. "Avalon. Elyria. Shambhala, Gahanna, Paradiso. You find them, or they find you."

I locate Priam below deck in our chamber, seated on the mattress and absently rocking the bassinet with one hand while the baby cries, his attention lost to a compass held in the other, his grubby notebook facedown beside him.

"I'm trying to figure it out," he says, "but this compass has five directions."

I pick Morning up—he is still a human of impulse and instinct, mostly; he doesn't yet know the specifics of what he needs, only when it's given to him or taken away. "If this boat is going to get anywhere," I say, "we have to do it ourselves." Priam furrows his eyebrows at the compass, at my suggestion. "I don't think Hugh knows what he's doing," I say.

"Who?"

"Hugh. Your dad."

"That's not his name. It's Liam."

A chill runs across my shoulders. "He won't tell me where he's taking us."

Priam fidgets angrily on the mattress; his response is that of being backed into a corner, refusing to interrogate what seems so obviously amiss, anger at his own confusion. "He found us, didn't he? Do you honestly think we would have made it out of that building on our own? We'd be dead if it weren't for him."

"That doesn't mean we have to commit to dying now."

Priam picks up the notebook, turns a page, and bites his lip. He looks up and meets my eye, as if finding his place in a script. Then he sets the notebook aside. Abruptly, he hurls the brass compass across the room, where it doesn't even offer the satisfaction of smashing. It is the most solid thing on this ship.

¤

A fitful night passes in which the waters soften—it feels like we're more adrift now than ever, that we've reached a place the waves don't even touch. The rain lightens.

I leave Priam in the cabin the next day and emerge onto the deck. His father is yet rooted at the helm. I have a vague idea to find where he's kept the food he brought aboard, but I don't want to ask him for it; I don't want to be riddled and suspect that the stores aren't there, that they never have been. Instead, I make my way around the perimeter of the deck, looking for a hatch, a burlap sack, some access to the boat's underworks, anything, aware of our captain's ever-watchful eye. I pause occasionally at the railing to stretch my arms or pretend to examine something—a chimeric sculpture, the lonely rowboat. I look out at the horizon and convince myself I see something there. The rain has let up into a sprinkle. I feel it on my neck and conflate it for the prickle of observation: they are the same thing, the same atmospheric disturbance.

I zigzag slowly across the deck, and when I'm directly below his father's post, I haul the door to the captain's quarters open with both hands, steal inside, and pull it quietly shut behind me.

A short set of steps leads down into a cluttered cabin lit by yellowed lamps. There's a low table, a bunk in the corner. A dim painting dominates the wall across from the steps. The objects arrayed around the room all fit the setting: an astrolabe, a telescope, a set of heavy tomes with the titles rubbed off their spines, a stuffed bird. I poke through a collection of maps on the table, only to find that they're roadmaps of different states, like you'd pick up from the automobile club before a road trip— Ohio, Kentucky, Indiana—maps that mean nothing in this context, that are just set dressing. The futility of our mission falls over me like a blanket, and my eyes rise in the faulty light to the enormous painting on the wall.

It takes a second for me to take the whole thing in, and then I recognize it: Géricault's *The Raft of the Medusa*, the mammoth nineteenth-century French rendition of one of the most disastrous boating accidents of all time. The Medusa—with a crew of four hundred—ran aground a hundred miles off-course, and by the time the raftful of crazed, starved survivors was discovered thirteen days later, only fifteen were left alive. The fates of the other 385 were left to vivid public imagination: drowned, killed by other survivors, left behind, or eaten. Géricault's painting depicts the moment when one of the survivors sees a distant ship on the horizon and climbs to the top of the heap to flag it down, the others gone to waste and dying around him. I remember reading about Géricault's obsessive visits to French hospitals to study dead flesh, the purloined limbs he kept for weeks in his studio to watch their decay, his painstaking scale model of the cobbled-together raft. The painting is a shrine to death, an ode to failure in the name of Romance. And finally, the name by which Priam's father jokingly introduced himself strikes its referent: de Chaumareys, the disgraced captain of the Medusa, whose incompetence and lack of experience caused the disaster, foretold the voyage's doom.

Around me, the hull of the boat creaks like a coffin. I realize that every brushstroke of this painting—of any painting we've done, each string in the orchestra, every choral leap and accomplished chord, every perfectly sinuous human form, all of it—they were each of them a flexing muscle, together a lineage of falsified tragedy, wounded pride, and shored-up ego: they weren't my stories. They were Priam's. They were his stories.

A spear of light opens in the center of the painting, and for a moment I think that it's combusting, that I've managed to will it into flames, until I hear Priam's voice from behind me: "What are you doing down here?"

He's a silhouette moving down the stairs. The air is close in the cabin, stifling. "I'm learning about your father's fixations," I say. "What are you doing down here?"

"Hey. I was looking for you. What's wrong?"

"Have you seen any of this?" I brandish a map of Kentucky, wave my hands at the painting. "It's insane. It doesn't make any sense. What is he planning?"

He rubs his eyes like this is a conversation we've had too many times, the air of a haughty second-in-command, as if the master plan is too complicated for me to understand. I picture his father's eyes behind Priam's, inscrutably on the horizon, leveling me into a static part of the background, a prop. I instinctively step back.

"Hey." That word again, that casual, pacifying word, that acknowledgment and scold. Priam reaches behind his back, and when his hand returns it's holding a glinting object up to me: one of my mason jars half-filled with dirt, a tiny green bud just breaking the surface. "Look what I rescued for us," he says, his face wide with broad, sloppy hope. "To start over. To raise between us."

"You"—my mind cycles for the precise word, finds it—"you idiot. Do you even know where Morning is?"

Priam's face crumples like a half-dried papier-mâché head after the balloon is prematurely popped. "I think he's with Dad? But—"

I push him out of the way, making for the stairs. I hear the sound of glass breaking in my wake. The sunlight on the deck briefly glares out my vision: suddenly the sky is bright blue and cloudless, everything is bleached dry and ossified, as if I've been underground for years. I turn and climb the stairs behind me to the pulpit where his father sits, the bassinet next to him, his eyes on the water. When he sees me, he motions me over.

"Your child has a touch of El Greco to him," he says. He lifts one of Morning's hands. "The slender fingers. Of course, most figures in the Cretan's work also had somewhat elongated torsos, only really achievable through a long period of malnourishment, but there's an innateness of body shape required; we'd have to see how he grows. Unless," he laughs, an experimental laugh, "you let him go without for a few weeks."

I lift Morning from the bassinet, swaddled in a pale orange fabric I did not provide for him, one that comes from a sixteenth-century palette—the hospital onesie is gone—and I descend the stairs, not looking back. At the edge of the deck, I begin to unravel the ropes that hold the rowboat in place, the boat's single emergency provision, scarcely large enough for two. Someone was always meant to be left behind.

Morning stirs in my arms. In the periphery, I see the captain rise from his throne. I'm already sweating in the sun, like fingers on my scalp, crawling down my forehead. I hear the door to the captain's quarters bang open. The front half of the rowboat dips forward as the rope disengages, and I realize that I've got the order wrong. I throw one leg over the railing and topple backwards into the boat, holding the baby to my chest. I land on my back between the two seats, and the loosened rope slackens further. The front of the boat drops, dangling from the side of the hull, then banging against it, sending a vibration through my spine. I steady myself and Morning on the bench, my stomach swooping, and I reach for the remaining rope coiled around the knob on the railing.

Priam appears behind it; he places his hand over mine and I see it's stained with dirt. I work my fingers around the rope beneath his palm and pull it loose, and I recognize that there's a part of him that resists grabbing me harder, that withholds applying this pressure, that realizes we have arrived at this end. I imagine him below deck, in the dark, frantically shoving dirt from the floor into the broken mason jar, the bud vanished in the mess, hoping desperately that when he emerged into the light it would be remedied, he would have captured it rightly after all.

When his father appears beside him on the deck, a shiver goes through me at the match of their profiles, Priam's face in his shadow. In the spike of his sudden presence, Priam applies the pressure he hadn't before, and wraps his gritty fingers around my wrist. I wrench the last loop of rope free and break from his grip. Priam recoils like a snake. There's a second of weightlessness as the rope unspools, and then the rowboat crashes into the water. My breath comes halting and frightened, my arm locked around Morning.

I quickly draw the paddle from the bottom of the boat and dig it into the water. I thrust it backward like a sword. The rowboat spins aimlessly and points perpendicular to his father's ship. Priam yells something behind me, but my ears are pounding, and I can't make it out. I lift the paddle to the other side and push again, propelling the boat forward. Morning reaches out from my lap, pulling at air. I continue the motion over and over, without paus-ing, shooting off into the erratic depths, moving in a long radial line, further and further away, off of his canvas and into my own.

Only when I'm totally sapped of energy do I stop pad-dling long enough to catch my breath and look back. The ship is small and distant behind me: it seems to float motionless and hesitant, like a toy, robbed of whatever doomed directional sense it once had, of its will to move at all. I turn back to the journey at hand.

Sometime later, as the sun falls away, my paddle drags against something solid, and the boat grinds unexpectedly to a halt. I look over the edge and see brick below the surface: a narrow ledge, and just to the left of it, a dark rectangular plot. Through the rippling water, it looks like it was once a rooftop garden, the plantings now loose from the ground or hanging by their roots, their leaves and fruits sprawled underwater like seaweed.

I fashion a sling for Morning with my sweater. Once I've nestled him within it, he turns immediately to look out, to take the world in anew. He reaches for the forms visible below the water, his fingers grasping in air as if testing their shape. He makes nonsense sounds, primitive language; he gives them their names. I step out of the boat and find that the water only goes to my ankles, that I can walk on the brick atop the narrow little wall, one trudging step at a time.

Before me, twenty paces ahead, a creature trots along the ledge as if on the surface of the water itself, leading the way: if it is Peter, or one of the other saints, I can't tell at this distance. Beyond him, rising over the horizon, past the glimmering fields of water, in the dusty pink light of evening I see the outlines of buildings pulling up, of somewhere else standing. It is like no work of art I've ever seen.

LAND

(for Graham)

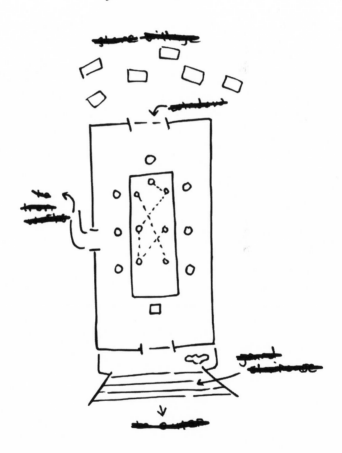

When we were come to where the thigh revolves
Exactly on the thickness of the haunch,
The Guide, with labour and with hard-drawn breath,

Turned round his head where he had had his legs,
And grappled to the hair, as one who mounts,
So that to Hell I thought we were returning.

"Keep fast thy hold, for by such stairs as these,"
The Master said, panting as one fatigued,
"Must we perforce depart from so much evil."

Dante

I WAS SUPPOSED TO be looking after a friend's huskies for the week while he was away for work. The journey to his cabin upstate was logistically complex—a four-hour train ride to a remote, infrequent bus, followed by a two-mile hike to the cabin, where the dogs had already been deposited—but my intent was to affect something simpler. In the trenches of the mountains, sheathed in forests of widely spaced pine trees, the house sat alongside a small, pristine lake; the word my friend preferred for this environment was "untouched," though he had built on the property there.

My friend, it was obvious upon arriving, had cultivated the house for purely aesthetic reasons. He'd built it himself, or had it built to his specifications, and you could tell its lack of deeper purpose just by looking at it: there was a fireplace that until I arrived had never been used, a lofted sleeping attic with a ladder, same, a vestigial well outside that I doubted had ever drawn water. My friend, who was also my landlord back in the city, visited the house with the dogs on weekends and always crashed on the couch, his time here spent shackled to his desk and power sources, shifting his nebulous property holdings around via laptop and occasionally appreciating the view offered by the broad windows as one might a landscape painting in a hotel room. The feeling of the cabin, therefore, was that of a model; the lake, as I've said, was a wonder.

This lake, which was no larger than any of the other area lakes and probably reached forty feet at its greatest depth, nevertheless struck me—perhaps because I'd left the city so rarely since moving there the previous winter—as a place of significant and potent meaning. Similarly, I tried to appreciate each aspect of my friend and landlord's second home during that week in a way that suggested essentiality, real purpose, and early-man necessity, and I dreamt of drowning in the lake before I'd even set foot at its shore.

The next day, when I did finally venture into the lake, still shaking free the vestiges of the nightmare, I misjudged my strength as a swimmer, and sure enough— as if succumbing to my mind's own grim prophecy—I almost drowned. The simple fact of it was swimming out too far too fast, that the journey to the center of the lake had been a series of easily surmounted small goals that added up to one larger, insurmountable goal, which was swimming back. But the romantic interpretation, and thus the version I preferred, was the one colored by the dream, in which I swam out there to recreate what I'd mentally experienced the night before, subconsciously or not so subconsciously seeking my own end.

Either way, while treading water at the lake's center, after I'd observed the cabin and surrounding mountains from this new vantage point, I realized that I was completely out of energy. I felt the lower portion of my body pull me insistently down. I tried to fight my way back to the shore, arms and legs burning, but I totally lost consciousness about two-thirds of the way across. Somehow, my body was carried the rest of the way, and I awoke later that afternoon, coughing up lakewater on the shore.

I treated this event like I treated everything I did while occupying the cabin, down to feeding the huskies the huge cuts of meat my friend stored in the freezer and taking the dogs on aimless, unleashed walks through the woods: like a spiritual experience, a dim referent to some vaguely pre-civilization part of history, where the sun had a godlike role and we ate what we killed with our hands, etc.

That said, my days at the cabin were necessarily routine, as the strict feeding and care regimen that my friend had left typed for me didn't allow more than an hour or two away from the dogs at a given time, and seemed specifically designed to restrict the three of us to the cabin itself, rather than to permit us to explore the land surrounding it. One of the dogs was sickly and required multiple injections per day; they were both prescribed vitamins that I needed to disguise and administer with their dry food, lotions I needed to rub behind their ears; there were either symptoms or side effects—*caution items*, my friend called them in his notes—for which I needed to closely observe; the cabin's plumbing and heat, likewise, needed maintenance and constant inspection. All things considered, it was clear that my friend did not see my time at the cabin as a holiday or a favor to me, but rather a contracted job, and that while I might enjoy and appreciate the early light and rustic finery of the cabin— its elegant pre-weathered furniture, the wild appeal of the remote landscape, its epically unchecked trees, the lake—my caretaking duties were firmly in service to the estate that my friend had created within it.

In turn, against his specific instructions, like wearing shoes indoors—and in apology to the huskies for their clinical routine—as I've mentioned, when I took the dogs out I let them go wandering off-leash, and this was eventually how I lost one of them. That night, as I strolled in idle circles a quarter mile or so from the cabin, searching for the missing husky with every faculty except my voice, I considered the breach in our friendship that would occur if I managed to permanently lose his dog during my week's sojourn at his cabin. I reached the conclusion that such an act would be irrevocable at the same time that I decided I'd done all that I could for the night, and I returned to my friend's—my landlord's—cabin alone.

On my way back, I stopped at the shore of the lake to examine, without touching, a group of narrow, pale shapes floating on the surface of the water, congregated at the lake's black edge like a cluster of lilypads. Kneeling, I thought I could see scales, or catch the glint of a sidelong eye, though it was too dark to tell for sure, and I resisted looking too closely. As I climbed back to the house, I somehow knew, with bizarre certainty, that these were the same creatures that had borne me safely to the shore the morning before; I must have been caught in their current. I shuddered at the thought of their slimy touch. I felt tapped by something powerful and celestial in a way I decided I was not poised to understand, the same mechanism by which you address any lingering, dubious circumstance: at some point, it becomes easiest, most practical, to stop thinking about it.

By the time I awoke the next morning, the dog had still not reappeared, and I'd forgotten which of the two had gone missing. Their names were Ares and Decatur, and I thought Decatur the sickly one; their coats had different patterns that I could distinguish when I saw them side by side, but by themselves, I had no idea. 7:30 arrived: first feeding. I broke up the vitamins and supplements and filled and stirred both their bowls as directed, set them in their usual spot, then watched the remaining husky pad forward and devour first the bowl for Decatur, then that of Ares. So surely this must be Decatur. I referred to my landlord's notes: Decatur was indeed the sickly one. But how could I be sure this was really him? How could I know that this dog was not his brother, and that he had merely gone to the bowl nearest to him? Would a wholesome dog have more of an appetite than a sickly one? I circled the cabin, performing my caretaker's upkeep: opening and closing faucets, checking temperatures, ensuring the pipes ran clear, that the cabin could sustain its idle operations for the day. Was it preferable to miss an injection, I wondered, or to receive an injection that wasn't necessary? Perhaps I could begin to administer the medicine and then gauge by the dog's reaction whether I should deliver it: if he went docile, as Decatur did under the needle, I could be assured that this was him. The dog lay by the fireplace; absent his brother, he had splayed himself evenly over both rugs. I called out both names to him. His ears flicked lazily in acknowledgment, but it was clear that I possessed no real power over him. How could I heal someone who did not want to be healed? The clock struck nine: terce. I had delayed much too long. I readied the injection at the sink. When I turned, syringe in hand, the dog was at my knees. *Do it*, he growled to me. And I had forgotten that morning's balms.

I fled from the cabin; I ran down the hill in the swelling morning to the edge of the lake. I pitched there and breathed. The creatures I'd noticed the night before had maintained their formation at the shore, pooling in the shallows, but in the daylight they had lost their shimmering magic—their color was now a dull, desaturated gray—and they did not react to me when I stepped into the water. There were more of them than I'd realized, a small school, at least fifty in all. They filled a considerable portion of the shore. I waded into their group fully clothed, the lake rising to my waist, and only when one brushed against my hip did I recognize that they were, in fact, enormous dead fish, unlike any lakefish I'd ever seen, their bodies long and narrow, each at least a foot in length, bobbing on the surface of the lake. They looked undeveloped, poorly adapted, like predators from a distant time: two small sets of fins and a disproportionate jaw with overbiting, flesh-tearing teeth, their skin mottled and bloated with time and decay. The wide, sightless eyes told me these creatures had once lived deep underwater.

Feeling suddenly overwhelmed by the arbitrariness of all the actions I'd taken since arriving at the cabin, I bent to pick up one of the ancient dead fish, but in so doing accidentally pitched forward, such that my feet slipped off a precipice in the shallows of the lake and revealed a cavernous depth beneath me—one that I'd somehow failed to notice during my misguided journey into the lake the previous day, or that hadn't been there—and I fell gracelessly into it, the startlingly heavy body of the fish twirling upward out of my arms like a missile as I slipped entirely below the surface.

I opened my eyes wide, and beyond the green murk, darkening as it descended, I saw nothing. From within, the lake masked its proportions. I blinked, my eyes adjusted to the water, and then faintly, through the haze, a thin, pale form unfurled from the distant below and lolled across my vision. I rose to take a breath, then pulled my head back down. When the bubbles cleared, I watched the form grow and, once it was revealed to be an appendage, multiply. Gradually, a figure began to take shape, drifting inexorably upward from a depth I couldn't hope to calculate, as if drawing toward me, something so big and ancient that in an earlier age it might have inspired song.

But the creature moved listlessly as it ascended, arms and tentacles splayed obscenely across the mantle like a flower opened too wide. And even as its size overpowered me, I knew without doubt that this animal, too, was dead, borne upward by some phantom buoyancy, a shift in the earth's deeper structure. I broke the surface over and over, gathering breath and watching the body rise by degrees, a few feet closer each time. I kicked my shoes off. Eventually, the carcass drifted to my right, toward the shore, and as the creature passed I was afforded a glimpse of one gaping, disintegrated eye, framed with waving white veins. To watch it stranded like this felt like a colossal failure of nature, as if I was witnessing something I shouldn't, some transitional moment that ought to have happened thousands of years ago, caught wedged between eras. When the body surfaced and crashed into the shore, the fish scattered and I was thrown backward by the massive force of the collision, landing on the rocky edge where I'd begun.

Grounded, I watched this wreck of early life on the shore, eerily quiet but for the residual waves pulsing through the lake. I climbed to my feet. The waterweight of my clothes pulled my skin south; I wanted it gone. The fish were strewn up on the land like regurgitated old bones, the squid a confused, glistening pink-and-gray mass at the center, its arms trailing in the water, a tentacle thrown over one eye as if in shame. It was as if some long-dormant vent in the earth had opened to release the prerecorded dead and pile them like clutter on the shores of the lake—and as always, I stared like a muted idiot at this sudden lack of movement, this accumulated stillness while my landlord's remaining husky probably went crazy inside.

I stepped into the water, as if approaching an entrance.

¤

As I've indicated, the owner of the cabin also owned the building where I lived back in the city, where I'd negotiated—meaning I'd been offered and had accepted—to pay twenty percent less rent for the month of September while for a week I stayed in his cabin gratis. The arrangement made no fiscal sense: our relationship, in its most basic and pragmatic terms, was that of serfdom, as I was still effectively paying him to dogsit at another property, albeit paying him less. But we tried gamely, mutually I think, to pretend that the financial component did not exist (for we had become friendly only after I became his tenant, though when we were introduced I hadn't known I would be his tenant, or that he was a landlord at all): I first wrote checks and then electronically deposited my monthly sum to him, and occasionally he would bring me a box of his favorite Korean fried chicken, or I'd ride with him in one of the luxury cars he rented through his membership service. I took these as acts of goodwill, as I believe—I still believe—they were honestly intended; I did not allow that I'd paid $1400 for the garish orange cardboard carton to sit untouched, vaguely slimy, in my refrigerator for a week until I threw it away, as I'd been vegetarian for six years. He was twenty-six years old, to my twenty-two.

His parents managed property, too—they had arrived from Istanbul when he was an infant—and my landlord had worked for several years in investment banking before he transitioned into landlordship full-time. He rented the building I lived in as a company called Narthex, which was also a startup, he'd told me, though I couldn't tell exactly what it did. I had asked, and over time the answer had changed or evolved, or maybe I was just presented with a different aspect of it, like a many-sided jewel refracting light: it was a property management company; it datamined real estate and property listings to allow analysis of market trends and opportunities; it was a program to analyze public land; it was a new platform for tenants to interact with their property managers (he never used the word "landlord"); it was everything.

The apartment itself was a 400-square foot studio on the ground floor of a three-story building in East Harlem. Before I moved in, my landlord had occupied the unit, and because I had little furniture of my own, many of his bachelor-pad trappings remained, an Ikea-heavy palette in black, gray, navy blue, and olive green. The floor was a yellowish, stained linoleum disguised with a few meager carpets, an upgrade I assumed he'd make after I moved out. A black couch dominated the entirety of the eastern wall; it was sectional, but there wasn't enough room to have it anywhere else, so its units were lined up in a long row, like seats in a waiting room. The northwest corner nearest the front door held the notched-out bathroom, which had been redone in gray tile while my landlord was living there. Fluorescent makeup lights were posted above the mirror, and the shower was a frosted-glass cube. Though the bathroom was the most recently treated area of the apartment, or perhaps because of it, this was the room most beset with problems. The ceiling had leaked for months and was now warped and bubbling in parts, but thus far I had failed to convince my landlord that the situation was sufficiently dire for him to address it. As such, I dreaded my interactions with the bathroom.

A tile counter with cabinets mounted above and below abutted the bathroom on the western wall, with a sink and fridge built in, though there was no oven or stove, only a hotplate that took up a quarter of the remaining counter space. I suspected that the kitchen pieces were elements of a kit, available at various tiers with different features, and that this was the lowest-end model, which assumed there was a stove and oven elsewhere. A black table sat apart from the kitchen, near the front door, matching chairs on two sides which hadn't been simultaneously filled since I'd sat there to sign the lease. The apartment's single window punctuated the western wall and separated the kitchen area from the bedroom area. In the back half of the studio was the bed, queen-sized and low to the floor on a black frame, also an inheritance. Beside it was a bedside table and a large, three-level shelving unit, like a display case, whose sides arched stylishly back into the wall, where I kept decorative items and books. Perpendicular to the bed-area, in the remaining space on the eastern wall that was not occupied by the couch, there was a closet in which a prefab storage system had been installed: it featured a pull-out shoe rack that could hold nine pairs, a pants rack, three drawers, and two quadrants for hanging clothes. Following the perimeter back toward the front door, mounted on the wall above the couch were individual adhesive components that formed a clock face. I hated this feature—its centrality in the apartment made it seem like a doomsday clock, as if it counted more than just daily circuits of time—but I didn't want to peel the little pieces off the wall in case it ruined the paint, and I didn't have anything to fill its place. Truth be told, even the display case beside the bed still held some of my landlord's possessions: a silver hamsa on a chain; a miniature buddha; a fold-out set of old Japanese woodblock postcards; a framed photo of an Ottoman ruin. The double-window on the kitchen side looked out on the empty, overgrown lot beside the building, which made it hard to be in the apartment without feeling visible to the outside, even with the curtains closed. Lying in bed, from a certain angle I could see through the window almost to the street beyond the fence, could watch people or cars move past as if through a crack into another reality. During low seasons, I could occasionally see into the building across the lot; a portion of the first-floor hallway, through which all entrants passed, was visible, as was one of the first-floor apartments, where two young women lived.

⌑

In the water, I crossed over the precipice again—the one I had missed the day before—and the lake opened up beneath me. For some reason, I was surprised anew, like a child that cannot grasp a simple illusion, and a delighted smile bloomed instinctively on my face. I swished my feet in the cold water, feeling nothing beneath them. I propelled myself forward, kicked several times more until I felt a faint burning in my legs, until I was sure that I was free of the shallow ridge in every direction. I caught one last look at the creature sprawled on the shore, an icy glare from one of the windows in the cabin; I spared a brief thought for the well-heeled husky and his doomed brother. Then I let my body relax. I quietly sunk from view.

As soon as my head dipped below the surface—like someone had slipped a bag over my head—I thrust my arms upward in a fanning motion, propelling the rest of my body downward. I drifted deeper. I stopped kicking my feet. I opened my eyes, suspended underwater. Dim blue blocks of color cut through the cloudy green surrounding me, like artifacts in a videogame that hadn't fully rendered. I could see nothing else around me: no shelf, no shore of rocks or plant life, just this blurry nothing, these looming edged depths my eyes couldn't make sense of. I repeated the gesture, pushing my palms up to force myself further down, my head tilted back to watch the surface above me recede. A ripple of light glimmered there, directly overhead, four wobbling parallel streaks like slats in a trapdoor. I had no conscious awareness of holding my breath. I pushed down again, distancing myself from the light, from the opening of the lake. The phantom shapes around me shifted in response to my movements.

It was as if I had found a ladder there, or had wrought one in the water itself, and each time I performed the motion, the pushing-down, I felt like I lowered myself a rung. As if my hands and feet had found purchase on some hidden structure within the water, and I was merely following it downward. The light above me dissipated. I felt a dull pain begin at my ear and then spread like a hand across my face; it itched vaguely. I tried not to inhale, to keep my mouth closed.

I kept climbing, down into the abyssal lake from which the creatures on the beach above had been vomited up. The darkly colored shapes adjusted, closing in as I climbed, and when I looked up again, I felt as though the water above me had become the sky, as if above an endless desert plain, its breadth so vast and unvarying as to lack volume or motion at all. It became cooler, then cold. Every so often something sifted against my skin, tiny flecks of errant matter drifted across my vision like dust, but I saw nothing else alive. The blue blocked in around me. I did not look down.

At a certain depth a fuzzing whiteness began to fill my mind; I heard it like static, crowding out the mental space I used for rational processing. Every few seconds a spasm of blinding terror would overwhelm me, and a stiffness skittered through my arms and legs, stabbed at my lungs, as if my body was realizing what was happening to it beneath this deceptive guise (a person climbing down) and lashing out to prove that it was still receptive. I knew that I was drowning, but somehow I also knew that I wouldn't drown *completely*, whatever that meant, until I reached the bottom of the lake, the end of this invisible ladder. I had a process to complete, and I could not die until it was completed.

Some unknowable distance down, I lowered myself another rung and my feet lost purchase—or the dissonance that I had created to convince myself of the purchase faltered—and I suddenly floundered. I gasped and took in a mouthful of water, and my hands scrabbled to find the ladder, but it was gone, or had never been there, or I could no longer believe in it fully. I was impossibly deep now, surrounded by inky blue. A deep rumbling rose in the water around me, and in my panic I thought it was the ragged sound of my waterlogged lungs trying to produce air, a death-growl. I stirred hopelessly at the water. I kicked numbly. I saw streams of bubbles arcing past me, their presence a reminder of the air that I was losing, that was draining from me like blood from a wound. I knew my panic was only making it worse, but I couldn't help myself: to remain still would seem like nothing, would be to passively accept my fate. I tried to remember the morning before, on the surface of the lake—I remembered my eyes sliding closed, almost in relief, as if the lake had lulled me into stupefied calm—but here they were now, open and aware and stinging, I couldn't close them: I had too much energy left in me, I was not at that threshold yet. I spun crazily, thrashing in slow motion; I somersaulted and inverted. I drifted, I kicked my legs. I saw a door.

It occurred at the same moment that I recognized the bottom of the lake: a basin of settled sand, smoothed surfaces of rock and hardscrabble plant life that had worked its way up through the cracks. Embedded within the sand and rock was a great, circular stone plate, its diameter at least the length of the living room in the cabin above. Seven circles were carved in a ring around its perimeter, and each carried a symbol that my blurry vision did not permit me to read. And I knew it was a door—or a gate, more properly—because it was ajar. A drift of sand was arced to the right of the stone plate, as if it had been rotated open at some point, revealing the channel beneath. But the gate hadn't closed completely, and on the left edge of the passage that it covered, there was a sliver of dark space, like a drop-shadow, where the plate couldn't re-set flush against the ground; something from the passage below had blocked it. That croaking sound, that failed choke I'd thought had come from my body—it had been the door grinding against whatever was keeping it open. The sound had gone now, though, and the door had stopped moving; it rested in place as if it always had. There was something wrong here, I thought again, insistently, forgetting that I was dying, that this was possible. There was a procedure, a *process* that needed to be carried out.

I dragged myself closer to the door, and my legs drifted upward behind me. I kicked forward and dragged with my arms. I was swimming! All of this time, I could have been swimming. Up close, the gap between the edge of the door and that of the passage was about as wide as I was, but it had been blocked by some dark, fleshy substance, dead matter I couldn't look at directly, like a clog in a drain. I felt sure that this was the place from which the school of spiny fish and the squid had emerged; there was some refuse chamber down here where they'd been kept. I pictured a stone kept atop a well.

In my curiosity, I'd forgotten all about the fact of my

drowning, and it seemed as though in this forgetting I was spared its physical reality; my fascination had saved me, or tricked me. I drifted closer still—the blockage seemed to have tendrils, or some part of it moved in the water—and in the closing distance I made out several of the symbols hewn into the three circles on the stone door closest to me: a face in profile, as one might find on a coin; a severed wing, like that of an angel; a Y-shape with minute branching offshoots like a tree, or bristling hairs. It was here—in trying to make out the other symbols, in this further distraction—that the drowning indicators abruptly returned. I choked, and the symbols went blurry again.

To the left of the circular stone door, separated by about six feet and partially obscured by a shifted layer of sand, wayward scraps of lakeweed, there was a planked wooden hatch in the ground, about three feet on each side. I swam frantically toward it, seized the iron handle at the bottom of the lake, and pulled.

It took a second to reconcile what I saw beneath the trapdoor. By all appearances, I was now looking down into an entirely separate body of water. A rippling square lay beneath the hatch, like the surface of a still pond recently disturbed. It was dark below—only the slightest light from the lake reflected in the surface—giving the illusion that the stuff in the hatch was somehow a different form of water, a different viscosity, maybe, or that there was a barrier between the two spaces that caused this effect.

I grasped the edges of the opening. My fingers grew cold when they broke the surface of that new water; it was at least ten degrees cooler than the water in the lake.

I wondered abstractly if I was now dead; the word "port-cullis" occurred to me, without definitional significance, and I pulled myself forward into the hatch. I heard a faint splash, a dunking sound as my head pulled through, or under.

I'd become so accustomed to the not-breathing-breathing that had borne me to this depth that when I broke the surface of that new water—like passing through a veil—my body braced in the frigid water and I instinctively took a breath, inhaling a mouthful of freezing lake-water, and the panic returned. I coughed, but there was no expulsion, only an inward rush of water. And now my body was facing blindly downward in the dark, and I could see nothing around me.

My arms flailed out to either side, brushed a craggy edifice. The trace of one edge multiplied my perception of others, and I became convinced there were obstacles all around me, that I was trapped in a tiny, rocky crev-ice upside down without egress, without enough space to turn my body—a trap! I kicked viciously, and one of my feet skimmed rock, but my rationality had departed again: I did not understand that this meant the surface was behind or above me, I thought it was beneath. I pushed off and hit my forehead on a rock, and the pain made me freeze up, so I might have drifted deeper, prone, and by the time I reacted and started thrashing again, I think I must have crossed the threshold into a wider passage, somewhere beneath, or alongside, or branching off in another direction from where I'd entered. My limbs spasmed randomly again, touching no surface, which for some reason was even more terrifying than being in an enclosed space: one way or the other, I was going to die in this chamber. But something—an anger—pushed me forward, and I dragged myself through the water as I felt the sensors across my body slowly, finally blinking off.

My forehead struck rock again—I fluttered from my body for a moment—and when we reconnected I heaved downward, scrambling through the darkness, swiping at the water with my arms like branches, like I was plowing through it. At either side of my peripheral vision, in that excited movement, two tiny spots of light appeared, then dipped, then swung up again closer together. For some automatic reason, I did not want the two lights to meet. I scurried through the liquid dark like a pursued quarry, exhausting myself, ceaselessly moving forward, as if I could push the lights apart with my body. I blinked, and they were right on top of me, like searchlights.

I breathed out—I remembered the expansive way my landlord had said "the cabin" over the phone, the exalted, breathy pause that followed those two words, as if by having it constructed he had thereby reconfigured the land around it into a single entity, as if "the cabin" dictated not merely a building in the woods but cabin and woods and mountains and lake itself—and I breached the water at the same time, as if through a door into a foyer, only to find myself again on a wet and stony shore, somewhere below it all.

¤

I had fallen asleep with my headphones in and the lamp on, and I awoke to the vibration of my cellphone on the nightstand. My landlord had texted me that he'd rented a Cadillac and would be stopping by in twenty minutes, if I wanted a ride. There was still music playing in my ears: the soundtrack I was listening to, for one of the Castlevania games, had been looping continuously while I slept. When I sat up I pulled the headphones out—my ears ached slightly beneath—but the melody had cemented itself in my head. It was shortly after seven in the morning, and I knew that twenty minutes to my landlord could mean ten as easily as it could mean two hours. Either way, in the blue morning light, there was little time to waste.

I jolted out of bed and made immediately for the bathroom. The soft, discolored water stain in the ceiling had spread beyond the bounds of the shower since my last inspection. A faint crease of water branched out from the amorphous, wet shape, crossing almost half of the bathroom; it held a dew, and the floor below was spattered with water. I found two towels and spread them over the floor. The cycling melody in my head—where was it from? the Royal Chapel? the Long Library? I thought that I should buy flip flops to enter the bathroom from now on. I skipped shaving, showered and moisturized so that my skin had a glow. I said to myself: *You are not going on a date.* But when my landlord texted me an hour later and said that he was out front, I stood from the long couch where I'd been waiting and walked out of the apartment and then the building—two doors that each used a single-code entry and through which my landlord could enter unannounced at any time, and had—dressed as if for a date.

These rides took many forms. We might share a meal, I might accompany him on some errand or to another property, or we might circle the neighborhood with the windows down, blaring hip hop: it was like I was being exercised, as one would a pet, but I was unable to resist the invitation. The rental was double-parked in the street—it was not hard to tell which car was his. I gestured to him through the window, opened the door, and slid into the passenger seat. The interior smelled new, and I, too, felt fragrant and untouched.

"How's it going?" he said. He was wearing his usual leather jacket, a white t-shirt beneath. He had described his haircut as "Danish"—it was short on the sides and swooped back up top, and had been maintained since he returned from Europe—but the aesthetic was truly more that of a dapper greaser. I hadn't seen him in over a month, but every time I did I was taken aback by his affability, his attractiveness, lulled into a kind of panicked receptivity, a frustrated non-action that prevented me from raising any issues with him. "You good?" he asked, rubbing my shoulder the way one would a young child at school pickup.

"Yeah yeah, for sure," I said, my voice ping-ponging between different registers with each syllable. "Where are we headed?"

"Just 86th street," he said, putting the car in gear and surging instantly forward. "I have the rental for another thirty minutes. It's just enough time to get us to the garage."

He turned the corner. One of the huskies was inexplicably in the backseat; he lunged forward at one point and grazed the side of my head with his nose. Was I intimidated by his success? Was I in love?

My landlord turned left and proceeded toward the FDR. "Did I tell you the good news?"

122

"No," I said, genuinely enthusiastic. "What's the good news?"

"We're gonna renovate the whole second floor of 372. I just got the final estimate."

372 was the building where I lived. "Just the second floor?" I said.

"For now, yeah," he said, seeming not to take my point, or to deftly ignore it. "New everything: hardwood floors, French doors, new kitchen. Like with your bathroom."

"Yes," I said. The dog's saliva dried on my ear; it would all need to be cleaned again. I had mentioned the leak to him many times before over the past several months— photos of the bathroom ceiling comprised our most recent text exchange, prior to this morning—and I knew I had to mention it again in person, to make the problem stick, to engage the process of its resolution. But how could I bring it up now, riding shotgun in his luxurymobile, when it already felt like he was favoring me, while we sped off toward pleasures unknown?

For the remainder of the half-hour he had left with the car—which we spent most of zooming down the FDR, alongside the East River—my landlord beguiled me with the tale of his trip to the TASER world headquarters in Scottsdale, Arizona that he'd taken the month before. It was unclear to me why he had gone there, whether the anti-death weapons manufacturer held for him a mysterious professional obligation or merely personal appeal. He had been given a tour of the facility, he said; they'd showed him the factory, the offices, the black glass enclosure that served as the secret design space.

"Check this out," he said. He pulled his phone from his pocket and unlocked it. His eyes left the road as he negotiated to the photos. The car felt expensively frictionless. Where was the other dog? He tapped the phone and handed it over. It was a photo taken looking up at the massive complex against the desert, whose towering edifice displayed translucent images of monumental police officers fully outfitted with TASER gear. "There's biometric eye-scanning just to get inside," he said.

"Pretty cool, man," I said. "Was the trip for Narthex?"

He let out an inscrutable beat of laughter. At the end of the tour, he told me, they'd brought my landlord down to the factory floor and ritually tasered him. He told me that all new employees had to go through this rite. I thought of it as a sort of hazing, into this fraternity of shock and awe, to which my landlord, feeling somehow akin, had voluntarily submitted. I was left wondering if he had built his visit specifically around this experience, if he had traveled and paid significantly for this one intense, erotic shock.

"What did it feel like?" I asked.

He bit his lip and sucked in. "I don't know how to describe it—it was so much more all-encompassing than I'd thought. Like my whole body blinked out for a few seconds—I was just a twitching ball of reactions, just like…raw stimuli. I lost all self-awareness and motor function. It was like being a—like floating in empty space. I was just suspended there, no threat to anyone."

He had totally gotten off on it. "Did it hurt?" I asked.

He nodded and smiled, and then shook his head, wistfully, I thought. "I honestly couldn't tell you."

We returned the car to the garage, less than forty blocks from where I'd started. He retrieved the husky from the backseat and leashed it. "What are you up to next?" I asked, on the sidewalk.

"Gotta head back to the office," he said, gesturing downtown. "You?"

"I guess just back home," I said.

"Cool cool," he said. The dog tugged him elsewhere, and I knew he would follow. The sun was now high in the sky. It was a Sunday morning. I felt stranded.

"Did you enjoy the ride?" he asked, wrapping the leash around his fist. He needed the affirmation, to know that I had enjoyed myself. But what, in truth, had he given me?

"Yeah, it was really smooth," I said, as if describing chocolate. "Luxurious."

He loosened, and the leash went slack; he gave me a brotherly hug. I flooded with something, and as we drew apart I said, my voice catching, "Are you going to address the leak in the bathroom?"

His face fell. I wanted to reach out—to touch him, to apologize, to change what I'd said. I would have paid dearly. "Of course I am going to address the leak," he said, and then my landlord and his dog were gone.

⌑

The lights resolved themselves as lit torches, mounted at eye level on the walls of a small cave. They crackled slightly, and beneath them I heard the water lapping behind me, my legs still dragged within it. I smelled damp earth and smoke. Where could it be escaping from? The rough floor gradually inclined ahead of me, and the cave widened before wrapping out of sight. The place glowed a soft orange, and craggy shadows cast about the floor. The ruddy walls glimmered with perpetual moisture. I pulled myself out of the water and climbed shakily to my feet.

The pool I'd emerged from was narrow and dark, tucked into a corner of the cave; had I approached it from this side, I wouldn't have considered that the water led deeper or elsewhere. I stood at the edge of the pool until the water stopped reacting to my body's former presence in it, until it had silenced itself completely and my breathing had done the same, until I'd readjusted to this soily underground air, trusted that I could still breathe at all. My upper half already felt relatively dry—I had no idea how long I'd laid there on the shore before I came to—but everything from my waist down felt hopelessly waterlogged and encumbered.

I dug my hand into my pocket and pulled out the black plastic heap that had been my phone. In my other pocket was my leather wallet, which now reeked and made a suctioning sound when I pried it open; everything inside it had matted together, but when I slicked the cards apart, I still recognized my face on my ID. I couldn't believe I had made it down here with all of these vestments relatively intact. Suddenly they seemed to me like irrelevant burdens, like weights I had tethered to my body to make it sink faster. I discarded them on the cave floor.

I trudged up the incline when all was quiet again. Just off the path, on a small promontory that looked out over some larger, deeper chasm, lit by torches on the far wall opposite, I found a small stone basin that stood at about the height of my belly button. It reminded me of a birdbath, though I knew that to label it a birdbath was to degrade its deeper purpose to some degree, but I didn't know by which other word to describe it. A washbasin. A bowl. Whatever its true name, it was filled almost to the brim with clear water.

I understood that I was to cleanse myself before I could proceed, that to go past this point in the same disheveled state in which I'd crawled onto the shore would be perceived, cosmically, as extremely rude.

I pulled both soaked shirts over my head and dropped them to the ground in a wet, coiled slop. I shivered and crossed my arms over my chest, rubbing my shoulders with my palms. I unclasped my belt and slid it out of its loops, put this to ground as well. My pants dipped slightly around my hips. I returned my arms to their cradling position. I liked this look of me, I saw it as if from afar: the way my arms masked my chest hair, the way I covered like a girl in a communal shower, the weight that I'd lost in the past ten months, the trace of rib that showed beneath my elbow, how my skin shined wet in the cave-glow, the plunge of the jeans at my hips—the strap of my boxers visible—maybe felt like it could be, like it could be *coy*, in reading. I felt, for a moment there, almost proud of what I had achieved. But I knew that I was still incorrigibly filthy by someone's eyes, and I still had to take off my pants.

The denim felt slimy from the lakewater. I unbuttoned my jeans and took them off with more deliberation than I had my shirts (I was already barefoot). I rolled them slowly down one leg and then the other—where the hair was thicker than on my arms—and the weight of the sodden pants was impressive. It felt good to be rid of them. I took the boxers off separately; I stepped out of them. The removal of the top half of my clothes had allowed a shifting of lenses, the lower half whatever the

127

opposite of that was. I felt shamefully exposed in lurid detail.

My hands dipped to cover my crotch before I stepped up to the basin. There was no reflection in the water there, and it was perfectly clear; I could see to the stony bottom of the bowl.

I sunk both hands into the water—it was cold and bracing—and raised my palms full to my face. I rubbed the water into my skin. I leaned forward and splashed more, scrubbing deep into the greasy crevices around my nose and eyes, the corners of my mouth, behind and inside my ears. There was a shimmering after-feeling that lingered on my skin for a few seconds, and the stinging in my forehead from where I'd hit rock underwater dispersed and vanished. I cupped a handful of water and sprinkled it over my shaved head, massaging it into my scalp like shampoo.

I proceeded like this down the rest of my body. I washed around my neck, my chest and stomach, down each of my arms and in each armpit. My back was difficult; I ended up flinging water over my shoulders and letting it run down. I rubbed water from the base of my calves over my knees and down each leg. I cleaned between each toe and the sole of each foot. I rinsed after every use. As I washed myself, the water gradually tinted, went from its pristine clarity to vaguely translucent from whatever shitty deposit the lake had left on me or which I'd had innately on my body, and I wondered about refreshing the basin's supply.

And I knew, inevitably, that I was going to need to clean my genitals, I was just going to have to do it. I left them for last; I bowed my legs out in a cowboy pose and did my inner thighs first, and then my buttocks. Then, finally, I dipped both hands into the basin (I could no longer see them when they were submerged), rubbed them furiously together, and addressed my junk. I pretended I was hand-washing a dirty sock in a sink, mashing it into itself and pulling it out, rolling the scrotum between my thumb and forefinger like I was trying to smooth it out. I ran the side of one hand up the crease between my buttocks. I realized that I'd been holding my breath the whole time.

I rinsed my hands in the now-filthy water, and upon drawing them out realized that I needed to wash them again, that putting my hands back in the water after massaging my crotch had turned the whole basin into dickwater, and it was going to be dickwater from then on out. I stood with my dripping hands held over the basin, pondering.

I looked back down the little slope at the water I'd crawled out of, which in this moment of logistical discord didn't look like lakewater, and seemed like it might be enough to be considered relatively clean, at least for my hands—it had to be. I abandoned the basin and walked back to the pool. I crouched down at the edge. I rinsed my hands with the undesignated water, and as I knelt there, I felt suddenly the overwhelming need to urinate. I forced the thought out of my mind by focusing on the motions of cleaning my hands, until I noticed that I was inadvertently rubbing the water up my forearms as well—my ordinary way of handwashing—meaning that I had now not only bathed my hands in the lower-quality water, I had also re-soiled my arms, too. *Shit,* I thought. *I am a fucking idiot.* And I still needed to pee, and I didn't know where I was going to do that because the cave seemed designed only to support interactivity in a few designated spots, and if I pissed in a corner, not only would it desterilize the entirety of the chamber— count against me eternally or karmically somehow—but it would probably lie there soaking for centuries, and there was that watchful eye wherever above. And I would need to clean my junk and then my hands again afterward, of course, if I was to proceed.

I stood up again at the edge of the pool, considering the mechanics of what I needed to accomplish and the levels of cleanliness involved. I thought of my hands, my genitals, the soles of my feet, a tingling spot at the back of my scalp. The basin and its gently lapping supply of dick-water. The pieces floated disjointedly through my head like an ill-defined logic puzzle. I had no head for business. There was this terrible pressure in my bladder, and I felt like if I didn't pee immediately, the stored-up urine would contaminate the insides of me and thus render the whole process meaningless. And what use was a clean outer body at the cost of a poisoned inner one? My head swam. I felt like there was an obvious solution that lay just out of my reach, that a smarter person would have arrived at instantly. Pool. Basin. Cock. Hands. Water.

I turned back and pissed into the stone basin; in the pool, I washed my dick and then my hands again. I turned once more to the torchlit path and proceeded up the incline and past the now utterly besmirched basin—a dizzying fear gripped me at the thought of looking over the edge of the promontory where it sat—and into the little chamber around the corner.

I was flummoxed when I didn't see a door in the cave

wall, or an entrance to another, deeper passage—the space was largely in shadow, since the torchlight didn't reach here—and I began to sweat: a watery layer of dubious cleanliness sprouted from the worst parts of my body. I had made a mistake somewhere, clearly, or taken a wrong turn. I wobbled on my feet. The air was very still around me. When I heard a faint grinding sound to my left, in a dark corner of the cavern, I staggered toward it frantically, tripping over the rocky floor, and there I found the hinges of a little wooden door, which I clawed open.

At first, I thought that the door led to an empty wall of the cavern, for I was greeted with another bare, rocky surface. I stood for a moment in shock and defeat, in trickery. Ducking my head inside, however, I found a narrow passage that led to the right, just wide enough that I could navigate it by scooting sideways. I wriggled, naked, into the confined space that it offered. I was almost instantly in full darkness, and as I shimmied carefully along—my chest, back, and knees grazing the stone to my front and back, one palm protecting my genitals—I thought about how just a few months ago I wouldn't have been able to do this, how navigating the narrow passage would have been an impossible and ridiculous demand: its confines felt designed to suit my new form.

The space continued for a long while, though because my movements were slight, it was hard to estimate how much distance I covered—a few hundred feet? Half a mile? In any case, as time passed and I edged deeper, I had the curious sense that the passage was curving gently, carving a wide arc—there was something in my constant readjustment that caused me to notice this—and when I detected this trace of a structure, I felt a stirring of purpose in my chest, as if I was skirting the edge of a larger darkness, as if I had somehow—by bungling my way forward, through will, through happy accident—avoided something dreadful or fearsome, had happened onto a path that would safely bear me to where I was meant to go.

Indeed, at one point a section of the wall behind me crumbled away; I felt a great stench of hot air on my back, and my periphery flushed orange. I nearly toppled, but there was a bar embedded in the rock that I grabbed to keep my footing, and I crossed back into the passage on the other side of the gap. I didn't look behind me or down. I continued bravely on into the narrow darkness, following the way as it guided me.

I had continued past this interruption for a while when, abruptly, my shoulder struck a wall on my right side, indicating that I could go no further, I had reached the end of the path at this level. The sting of the rock sent a surge of anger through my body—I had been betrayed! Led here to die!—and I fumbled for a moment in disorientation until my hands found the metal rungs of a ladder before me, anchored into the stone: another ladder, this time ascending. Why not stairs? Would not the space have been more conveniently served with stairs?

I could scarcely bend my knees given the width of the passage, but eventually I mounted the lowest step and negotiated myself up rung by rung, my legs slightly bowed out, my crotch held carefully away from the stone, occasionally using my shoulders and back to support myself against the opposite wall. Whenever a tender part of my skin brushed the rock unexpectedly, a wave of shock rushed through my body from the point of connection, like the ripples of sonar, and the feeling was so intense that I was sure this could be sensed elsewhere, tallied, each time I was touched.

As I climbed, a low blue light began to bathe me in its glow, and I knew that I was growing closer to open air. I hit my head at the top of the ladder, clenched my jaw in rage, and found a slatted cover above me. I shoved it aside, revealing the night sky. I clambered out as if from a manhole, like I was a trespasser creeping from the sewers of a great kingdom, seeking to blend in. I emerged into the night.

¤

A rocky field stretched out before me at a slight downward incline, coated in blue moonlight. I had arrived beyond the outskirts of what looked like a sprawling village of little stone houses, scattered across the landscape. At the center of the village, perhaps a half-mile from where I stood, a complex of obsidian black loomed above the stone houses, as large as a mansion. In the centermost building, a wide stair led to a brass-colored set of byzantine double doors. A pale moon hung above it all, the village and the castle and the land, or what could best be described as a moon, for it was a glowing, bluish orb that floated in place in a direct line above the keep, casting its light over everything in darkness, connected by a faint beam of light to the central building. Only the black structure itself seemed not to reflect its light, and the building's outline stood starkly against the night like a cut-out onstage.

Most of the houses lay solemn and darkened, though

sprinkled throughout, I noted a few that were lit from within. They were each roughly-hewn, and clustered closer together the nearer they were to the keep, like peasants swarming a breadline. I sensed a power relationship between the little houses and the keep at the center of them—an imbalance.

In the reaches of the sky to my right, far past the black fortress, a dot of white light suggested a guiding star, other than the moon the only visible object in the sky. To my left, on a distant hill, there sprawled an ancient tree, whose branches shimmered with an unearthly magic and drooped with fruit that shone like purple jewels, offering its own light. Behind me, more rocks: hemmed in by mountains again, I thought. But it was the black keep that beckoned.

Despite the scarred and haphazard makeup of the village sprawled around that keep, when I looked to my right at ground level, a hundred feet or so away, I saw what looked like a deliberate path worn smooth or paved into the rocky terrain, marked at intervals on either side by little stone cairns and huddled monuments. In one direction, it led toward the center of the stone village, presumably ending at the keep. In the other, behind me, the path gradually sloped down into the rocks and out of sight, below or between the mountains, like a valley carved by water. It was so clearly meant to be a road that the fact that I'd arrived beside it rather than upon it—combined with the relief I'd experienced as I edged my way through the passage belowground—made me immediately suspicious of its intent. Clearly, it led back down to whatever had lurked beyond the stone basin, the threat I'd successfully avoided. The apparent legitimacy of the path—whose bordering statues, I realized as I grew slowly closer, were of humanesque figures writhing in fabric—was itself a deception, meant to trick me into following it.

It felt inevitable that I would make my way through the village and toward the keep—I had already walked some distance from the hatch where I'd emerged, and there was nothing of consequence to either side of me save for the glowing tree, too distant and untouchable to seem properly real—but I felt stubbornly that I should not use the road to do it. Instead, I tracked the path at a distance, eyeing it warily as I followed it in parallel into the village.

The mystical tree slipped from view behind the looming black complex. As I picked my way across the rocky plain in my bare feet, through a rough alley between stone houses as far as possible from the central path, I took note of their uniform structure, which wasn't much more than a misshapen box, a doorway notched on one side, slot-like windows. Most of the houses were marred in some way, their entryway scorched or the roof blown out, and rubble often obscured my path. As far as I could tell, there was nothing inside them, no furniture or life. Intermittently, the smell of smoke wafted through my nostrils, as if to confirm my speculation.

In the distance, something—a strange, fiery light—popped off brightly and slowly rose in an arc to join the glowing core in the sky. I shielded my eyes as the orb-like moon pulsed and brightened in acceptance, and in the faint blast of energy it released, I saw the traces of dark constellations illuminated in the sky beyond it, patterns tricked by the atmosphere, like stars that hadn't been switched on yet. My eyes wandered to the distant star in the north (for I had decided that I was walking west, as that was the direction the window of my apartment, and the cabin, looked out): this star, too, seemed to grow infinitesimally brighter, but I could make out none of the terrestrial features below it, it was still too far off and faint, and the land in that direction was fully masked. I figured the two celestial objects were related in some way, that they shared an energy. Without quite knowing how, I had crossed the full breadth of the village, and I found myself at the base of the steps to the keep, looking upward. I heard another explosion, closer at hand, and when I turned, I caught another of the glowing, fiery lights moving upward along a preset trajectory through the sky, as if by gravitational pull, eventually absorbed by that strange moon.

Upon looking down, I realized how directly I stood in the light upon the steps—how much I might have looked, without proper context, as if I had approached the keep directly in order to throw open the doors. I quickly ducked off into the shadows on the southern side of the entrance. No particular plan in mind, beneath the stairs I found a stone archway masking some other passage, and without meeting any barriers or exerting any direct effort on my part, after three short turns down a stone corridor I found myself inside the keep, in the dark.

The underworks of the keep approximated a maze-like basement or dungeon: the walls and floor were stone and were interspersed with cells or cages and meandering prison-like corridors, all empty. Torches marked the walls, as they had in the cave, lit by an unseen hand. The area was silent and strangely absent of adornment, of any kind of accumulation or furniture or signs of habitation; the rooms were totally bare, even of dust, as if they'd been constructed recently but never used, like the basement of an unfinished house. Or maybe they existed, I thought obscurely, just to fill space, to create the appearance of purpose. I walked through this place for a while, trying to make some larger survey of it, to assign meaning to the grid-like network of unlocked gates, wooden doors, empty corridors, metal bars, and open doorways, but the logic of it, assuming such logic existed, was beyond me. At first I let the torches lead me, thinking they might be laid out to guide a visitor down a certain path or to illuminate specific areas. But their layout, too, was so methodical—every ten feet, there was a torch—as to resist classification.

At the far corner of this basement level, I found a rough stone staircase that wrapped out of sight. I followed it upward as it twirled, passed through another arched door, which I had to pull open, and found myself beside a great red staircase in a foyer finished in elegant marble. The ceiling was lofted high above me. The place was grand, outsized in proportion—banners of flat color hung from the walls as if in royal welcome, and the carpet shined like velvet—but I had the same feeling in this overly decorated room as I had in the bare cellar: this was no place where anything lived, but a figuration that masked something, a stand-in mimicking a shape that I was meant to recognize or ascribe meaning to, that I should find functional.

I imagined that the central staircase continued from the broad stairs that I'd elided outside, and indeed there was another landing down the stairs to my right, as well as a large arched door carved in swirling figures, through which, I suspected, I might have otherwise entered. In the other direction, to my left, the stairs climbed another level or so: at their end, following a small landing, there was another narrow door marking a marble wall. Across the landing from where I stood was yet another door, identical to the one I'd just entered through. I figured that this door merely led down to the opposite side of the basement from which I'd just emerged, but this didn't stop me from crossing to it and following the predictable winding stairs down to the bottom. I retraced my former route through the empty cells and stone corridors with an ill-founded and almost desperate anxiety, as if I was expecting to find something here I hadn't before, or to be faced with an obvious inconsistency that I would be forced to address (meaning, of course, that I was looking without truly looking, and had already committed to some degree to the idea that I would find nothing), until I had renegotiated the floor at least twice over and worn the potential completely dry. And with that, upon once more reaching the staircase where I'd originally ascended, I doubled back and climbed the other staircase instead. By the time I entered the marble foyer for the second time, I was tired and sweaty, tired and sweaty and naked at that, and had further conditioned myself—as I finally trudged up the grand carpeted steps, my hands on my knees, stopping to recover briefly on the landing before the door, which was flanked with erotic statues— to expect nothing when I opened it, as if a realtor checking a box on a long and unexciting list.

I did not immediately resolve what I saw beyond the door. It was a large, peaked white chamber, at its center a long and ornate table, and in the eight seats around it sat seven beings; I can think of no other word to describe them. Each wore a golden robe draped over a body roughly the shape and formation of a macro-human—I imagined each to be ten or twelve feet tall when standing—and in the shock at what I suddenly beheld, the first feature my eyes took in besides the fact of their presence itself were their gray hands resting on the surface of the table, which mapped to them an aspect of human design and thus colored the rest of my reading. I followed the hands into the golden robes, flowing over the chairs in which they sat, but where a head should have been, instead each had a different shape in its place: a branch of flame; a glistening, fleshy pink flower with its petals drawn back; a nest of black coils belching smoke (which I shuddered to see).

I seemed to catch them in the midst of some game. Before each on the table sat a goblet. One by one, in some preordained order, each picked up their goblet and poured some of it into their neighbor's, or into another goblet across the table. At the moment that the two liquids combined, the recipient would change slightly, as if in reflection of the one who had poured it. The being at the head of the table—its pupils blank, its white marble features frozen, among them all the one that appeared closest to human, and therefore with which I automatically sympathized—poured a dash of his goblet across the table to his left (I unconsciously assigned the being this gender on stately facial construction alone, because it had the bearing of those stately Greek statues)—into the goblet of the fleshy flower. The flower spotted white cysts in response, twitching slightly. The being with a branch of flame above its robed neck poured some of their drink into the goblet of the black orb, like an eclipsed sun, which sat two places down on the right. The black void pulsed forth a ring of light—a coronal ejection—that hung in the air like rings around a planet, a halo.

Instinctively, I shrank from the doorway where I'd entered. I did not want to be detected, to be involved in whatever was playing out before me. I treated them like machines, like automatons or consoles, as if they wouldn't notice my presence unless I interacted with them directly, even though every one of the seven seemed to stare at me with whatever semblance of a face that it possessed: a feathery ball with a beak-like protrusion, a mass that approximated a wretched hairball one might find in a shower drain. Opposite the white marble figure, at the head of the table closest to me, sat an empty chair smaller than the rest. In turn, I realized that all of the seven were hunched peculiarly in their chairs; the table seemed two or three feet too low for them, and they had to crane down over it as one would a board game.

The back of my scalp tingled. I swatted a phantom sensation off my hands. I felt the need to cover myself, and I turned toward the wall, cupping my hands over my crotch. I thought abruptly: *I am unclean.* The room had no other doors, but on the far side, beyond the table, there was a set of windows through which played a moony blue light.

I edged along the length of the room, hugging the wall. The beings tracked me with their sightless gaze, all the while maintaining their strange game. The fleshy flower sprouted hair, and then a long beak. The hairball began smoking quietly. The marble head remained, as far

140

as I could tell, the same. They turned in their seats to silently follow my progress. I looked back to the door where I'd entered: next to it stood a coat rack where a golden robe hung alone. I felt doubly naked. Suddenly realizing the advantage of my relative size, I dashed from the wall and scurried under the table like a chased cat. The beings had no feet beneath their golden robes (I wondered idly if they had taken this form to appease my human understanding in what small way they could), but some stump-like protuberance kept them balanced, and I figured they couldn't give chase. I crawled the length of the table on my hands and knees, emerged at the far end of the room—at the head of the table on this side sat the marble-headed being—and fled out the window. I hung from the ledge for a moment, exposed, realizing that I was outside again—I felt a breeze, or faked a breeze—and then dropped some feet to the ground below.

¤

I awoke that morning with the need to shave my head. I was shocked that I hadn't considered it before. I scampered down the ladder from the bed, retrieved my suitcase from the closet, and dug out the electric shaver that had sat untouched since I'd moved to the city. I heard faintly the sound of panpipes around me, and felt briefly dislocated—as if I'd tripped into some alternate universe—until I turned and saw that it was my phone, lying on the floor, the headphones yanked out by my sudden rise from bed, looping the Ocarina soundtrack.

I slid on my flip flops, braced myself as I opened the bathroom door, flicked on the light, and squelched inside.

The leakage, at this point, was still primarily relegated to the area above the toilet and in the shower, so I was able to stand at the sink relatively isolated from the decay, only remembering when I shifted my feet and heard the sopping towel burble beneath me. I needed to replace it. Over the sink, I used the scissors from the toolbox to cut my hair short so that I could more easily buzz it off. I pulled it out in vague fistfuls, eased the blades of the scissors in and rocked them back and forth, cutting it like a thick stem. I moved erratically across my scalp, without method—I realized, too late for correction, that if I'd proceeded more carefully I might have unintentionally arrived at a style I liked better than none at all—but my accomplishment was impressive, the volume of hair on my shoulders, in the sink and on the floor, and I felt an emotional weight lessen slightly at the change. When I left the apartment I would be different, visibly different, than I'd entered it, and this comprised the progress of a day: a change that would take months to completely undo.

My phone vibrated four times on the sink, startling the scissors in my hand. I set them down, no damage done, and picked up the phone. There were four texts from my landlord: "Dropping by your hood in half an hour—wanna grab lunch?" / "10 minutes" / "are you around" / "??"

A complex panic instantly enveloped me: my scalp crawled with sweat, and I felt my heart rate spike. The texts had arrived all at once, but each seemed more insistent than the last, as if they had been delivered minutes apart, anticipating my response. Had my phone lapsed in reception and only picked the messages up all at once, however long after they'd been sent? How much time did I have left? Wasn't my neighborhood more properly *his* neighborhood, because he owned the building that I lived in? Were there other texts that I had missed, other communications as a whole? Was he upset with me? Did he think I was upset with him? Why did he so eagerly want to see me? The questions raced dizzily through my head.

I fumbled out a positive reply, leaned my head over the sink, and rubbed the remaining cut hair from my head. It sprinkled into the sink. I ran the water and washed my face, no doubt creating horrible clogs in the drain—infinitesimally flecking his property with damage—and ran my wet hands through my hair, inadvertently spiking the difficulty of any half-measure job I could have done with the scissors. I looked like an infant awaiting its first haircut, an anime character. And now I needed to piss, too; I hadn't used the bathroom since awakening, but with the bathroom in its current shape, it was at least a five-minute process from end to end. I would have to get the umbrella and commit to dealing with the other half of the room. And with every second, my landlord zoomed closer.

I opened the cabinet above the sink for the bottle of Wellbutrin stored there, but in my haste I knocked it over, and the bottle spilled from the shelf—I must have misapplied the lid the morning before—and a half-month's worth of pills showered into the wet and hair-spotted sink, rolling toward the drain or fusing into place, dissolving slightly on contact. "Fucker!" I cried, gingerly scooping them out as best as I could, my shaking fingers quickly stained with powdery white. I laid the decaying

143

shapes out individually next to the sink. Their residue streaked down the basin. I picked off the stray hairs where they had stuck to the pills, flicking them from my fingers to the floor, until the task seemed both too fruitless and exhausting to continue. Around the stopper of the drain, mingled with clogged hair, several pills had fused together into a chain-like shape, like a protein—a business week's worth—and I tried to edge it free with my forefinger, trying not to disturb their construction, hopeful that I could save them all. But I had overestimated the strength of their liquid bond, and the chain broke, and at least three of the pills tumbled slimily into the drain.

I felt dangerously close to tears. My throat trembled, and I saw in the mirror my face had gone red, but I didn't want to know the extent of what I'd lost; I couldn't bear the thought of knowing how many days I would lose to the indeterminate fog that came from missing a pill, or how much energy and time I would waste wondering if that fog really existed, if it could really manifest itself so tidily in the pocket that 300mg could fill, or if I was just psyching myself into it, and whether I had more control than I thought, for surely—I knew immediately and certainly—I would not touch the extra pills that I had, the leftovers from previous days that I'd missed, because the fog, the lethargy wouldn't be severe enough to make me think that I should waste the extras, the ones I was saving for an unspecified Bad Time that I felt sure would arrive one day, sometime when I would need to take them all at once or something, maybe, or for when my prescription ran out and was not refilled—a long winding-down process, engaged before I knew I would be ready. In the moment I ran out, I would either believe in their effect totally or not at all. I felt almost physically the presence of my landlord, gaining on the building, drumming his fingers on the steering wheel. I blasted the faucet, ensuring a watery death for the pills stuck under the stopper. I rinsed my face again. I picked the most misshapen from the collection of bulbous pills on the counter and swallowed it, or it dissolved mostly in my throat, leaving a chalky aftertaste. I shook my head involuntarily from the bitterness; I shivered and restored feeling down the rest of my body.

I exited the bathroom and was halfway across the kitchen before I realized I was still wearing the disgusting flip flops. I kicked them behind me and crossed to the closet while simultaneously stripping: I got out a pair of jeans and a red t-shirt that I had never worn, figuring that our interaction wouldn't be long enough for my sweat to noticeably bleed through. I was surprised, briefly elated, that the shirt fit. I heard my phone vibrate from where I'd left it in the bathroom. Once, then again, then again: it was ringing. Adrenaline flushed through my chest. I had expected to hear the doorbell. I had planned to be greeted. I ran back to the bathroom and grabbed the phone from the counter, stepping back into the kitchen to answer it while realizing with a dismal sinking feeling that my bare feet were now wet with leakwater.

"Hello? Hello?"

"Hey. I'm out front."

"Okay. Okay! I just need to put my shoes on."

There was a pause—or I imagined a pause. "Okay. I'll see you out front."

I tugged socks on—they were soiled the moment they

touched my clammy, damp feet—tied my shoes, and made for the door. I glanced at the clock face on the wall: it was 10:20 a.m. Who the fuck ate lunch at 10 a.m. on a Sunday?

A sleek black Camaro waited in the street beyond the gate, and the restaurant ended up being the diner one block south, though it took us almost five minutes to drive there. "Can you believe I had to go all the way to Chelsea to pick this up?" he said.

Over his omelet, a breakfast food, my landlord related that he had been named one of the ten most eligible bachelors in the city, based on results tabulated from a new dating app where, in a well-publicized twist, women rate the men they've been on dates with. As a result, he was being written up in the city paper. He slid his phone across the table, allowing me to scroll through his charming email answers to the interviewer. All of his responses, he explained—hovering over his phone as I read like a proud father, his hair nearly touching my spiky fringe— all of them were carefully calibrated moves against his current girlfriend, over whom he fretted and dallied and subtly fed excuses to leave him.

"You'll see that for 'describe your ideal date,' I wrote, 'spend a day spontaneously exploring a city in Europe.' Now when Mira reads this, she'll think that I'm talking about when she came to visit me in Paris this spring and we took that trip to Florence. But in fact," my landlord said, raising a finger, "that wasn't truly spontaneous. I planned it weeks in advance. I'm actually referring to the French girlfriend I had in Paris, Therese, who invited me with her to Berlin one day, two weeks after we met. She bought the train tickets that morning and everything,"

146

he said. "That's the one that really digs the knife in."

I did not acknowledge his trick because at the moment, sitting in the booth, I felt like he was playing one on me, too. But like Mira, I would never be able to discern exactly what that trick was. Would he not admit that this was brunch, at best?

"You got a Narthex reference in there," I said.

He smiled. "Of course," he said. "I wouldn't miss a press opportunity like that."

Now, I thought, when tenants googled their management company, they would find not only the link where they could deposit their rent, but also this profile of their fuckable landlord.

He picked up his phone and squinted. "Oh shit, I should go." He signaled for the check. "Do you want to stay?"

I was being stranded again. I stood with him, he shrugged on his leather jacket, and we exited the diner. As he climbed into the rental car, he told me that his parents were coming to visit. He said this facing away from me, but I only nodded in response. He said, "They're looking forward to meeting you," and he pulled the door shut and drove off. I realized only as his car pulled away from the curb that he had not acknowledged my hair, had not appeared to have noticed it at all. It hadn't been enough.

¤

When I climbed to my feet, I found myself again at the edge of the stone village, which I now realized surrounded the complex—or fortress, or castle, or keep, whatever it was—albeit on the far side from where I had entered. The village was still bathed in the blue glow of that strange, ominous moon. I walked down toward the houses again: up to my left I saw the presiding tree on the dark hill, redolent of mythic intent, and to my right that far-off, guiding star in the sky. I felt as if I had made progress toward something, indescribable as it was.

Before I had gone far, behind me I heard a faint thwack against stone, and I turned to see that a knotted rope now hung from the window through which I'd fled. I turned back to the task at hand. A faint explosion echoed somewhere distant, and sure enough, a few seconds later the blue cast around me brightened in response from the orb. I felt as though I had achieved an understanding of this place. It was like a clock, I figured. The moon-tethered black fortress at the center of its face, the tree at ten or eleven o'clock. I had entered at, say, six. In affirmation, I looked over at the guidestar at one-thirty. Below it now, I thought I could discern the outline of a spire, the topmost peak of a much larger structure, still almost completely shrouded in darkness. And what kind of rocks might these be, I wondered, stooping to run my hand over the ground. Rough in some areas, smooth in others, gravelly in yet others—but of course I'd never been able to tell one variety from another. Standing, looking further afield over the rocky plain, it was impressive how much area the village covered. The stone houses went on as far as I could see.

As I walked deeper into the village proper, I noticed one of the stone houses off to my left was illuminated violently from within, and tongues of flame flickered at the slotted windows. There was a roar, like that of a large animal in pain, a beast struggling at its chains; it started throaty and vicious but ended on a clear, high note—the hint of a plea, of begging. Since I was fairly close, and still resting on my laurels to some degree, I thought that I should investigate it, in the spirit of gathering more information about this strange yet seemingly ordered place.

I wound my way toward the thrashing house, keeping a watchful eye. Like the houses on the other side of the keep, nearly all of the stone houses here were damaged, blackened by fire or collapsed entirely. They looked, I thought now, assembling pieces in what order I could, as if they had exploded from within. And as I neared the lit-up house, the rest of the village motionless around me, empty and dead silent—not so quaint as I'd painted it at first—I wondered if whatever or whoever was trapped inside was soon to suffer the same fate. I looked to the sky, where that glowcore seemed to loom, its intentions unknown and therefore questionable, leeching energy from the impoverished village below. I felt the heat from the house on my skin, a class angst. I heard the pained howl again; it seemed to address me directly. Flames licked from the windows and entryway—in desperation.

I remembered my friend's husky, bounding unleashed into the forest. I pictured the fine cuts of meat in the fridge of the cabin, wrapped in wax paper. Who had put them there? How had they reached the cabin, and why could this phantom not have watched the dogs instead of me?

I approached the doorway through which the fire raged. I was brazen, like flame itself: the heat was intense, the light brighter still, but I didn't consider that I could be burned or wounded by it. I'd arrived at an instinctive understanding that I existed beyond such things at this point.

So I entered the house, where the fire blazed white and yet there was no smoke: it was like stepping before some eternal, holy light that existed beyond human sensory capacity. I was blinded, briefly, as if I had entered an incredibly deep space, or an incredibly wide space, like facing something that was beyond dimension or intake, even sight, like a dream of dying. But then, rudely, I felt an awful sizzling on the surface of my skin, over the entire front of my body, and I heard a wave of crackling. A foul smell rose to my nostrils, of burning hair.

I recoiled from my own stink, my front half searing, weeping madly, and slowly regulated the span of the room, separating the bucking shape in front of me from the light it emanated: a writhing figure shackled to an iron frame by its arms and legs. The figure was proportioned like a slightly magnified human, seven or eight feet tall, and bulkier, as if wrapped in heavy coats. A matted crown of hair hung down over their face, and their arms and legs strained against the mechanism that bound them in place. Their—*his*, I thought resolutely, in species sympathy—his entire body was enveloped in flame. He roared and struggled, and when he flung his head back I saw a monstrous, leathery face, scarred and deformed—I thought of a scarecrow or a Picasso—and he howled at me as his torment increased. Flaps of skin were missing in patches across his body, sleek pink and black flesh where it had gone, his remaining skin like packed layers of rough clay or smears of muddy color in an old oil painting, the meat of his body crumbling piecemeal into an ashy pile at his feet. He was burning alive before my eyes: dying. Here I stood, invincible, while this figure died in front of me. I choked with the weight of my responsibility—if I didn't act, I would be abandoning what remained of my humanity, I would no longer deserve to be content.

I unclasped one of the restraints that bound his arms to the frame. It was a simple latch, and the cruel efficiency of it shook me, the brutal elegance of the restraint: it was designed to snap closed when weight was applied. There had been no chance for him. When the shackle fell open, the figure's arm went slack. He paused and flexed his giant's fingers, aware that something had changed. I crossed his girth, knelt at the restraints by his legs (spring-loaded beneath the heel; ingenious, monsters, I thought) and freed one of his feet, which looked like great leather sandals, thick volcanic slabs of meat. But as I stood to address his other arm, he raised his great foot and planted it in my chest.

I careened backward across the room and collided with the stone entryway as the figure broke free of the remaining shackles with an anguished roar. On the ground, back weltering and breath gone, my sympathy washed out of me for a moment—I was indignant at the rejection, furious. I saw the panels in the ground below its feet—how long had it even been held captive here? The figure fell to its knees. A pair of nubs below its shoulders writhed like blind worms seeking light. A massive fleshy backpiece sloughed off and dissolved—five minutes of suffering? Ten? And then the beast bolted forward on all fours—for that was what it must be, a beast of instinct, of no loyalty—I rolled aside, and it rammed its mighty shoulders into the doorway of the house, then again, and again until the wall collapsed around me, and then it galloped into the endless space beyond, flaming into the night.

I struggled to my feet and ducked through what was left of the ruined doorway in time to see the beast tear southward across the landscape toward the hill, already impressively far away, the fire glowing off it like a beacon, pulverizing little stone houses in its wake. For a few moments, it seemed as though a beam of light from the moon above followed the beast, attached to its back like the sightline of a sniper rifle, and then it faded out of existence. The sky dimmed a little. The beast crested the hill and set the ancient-looking tree ablaze. The flames quickly swamped its trunk and engulfed the upper branches, which bowed and dropped their shimmering fruits to the ground. They splashed viscously apart and vanished in a sizzle. My heart sank a little as I watched it go; I felt unthanked.

I looked up at the sky, at the moon glowing there, and for the first time—maybe because I had stared so hard at the flaming beast in the house, because my vision had recalibrated to detect past a certain level of brightness, or the light itself had dimmed enough to allow a closer look—I noticed that there was a structural formation above the orb, that faint lines connected to form a peaked ceiling, like that of a chapel. I had assumed—everything I'd witnessed had relayed to me—that I was outside, but there was the ceiling. Again, I felt betrayed by what had been offered me—misconstrued.

In the peripheral glow, I connected the lines on the ceiling, forming shapes and figures. What I had seen before as constellations, when I'd assumed that the space beyond was sky, were actually carvings or paintings, like what you'd find in a museum or a house of worship. I squinted to discern them in more detail, but the area around me was growing darker, and the giant bulb itself quickly faded in luster, masking the area above it in shadow once again. I looked back to my own level as the stone houses around me retreated into darkness. Only the tree on the hill to the southwest glowed, aflame.

I looked down and realized my front half had been rendered completely hairless by the fire in the house. In the distance, I heard the crash of the beast bashing into something; in time, as I stood there dumbfounded and confused, the once-glowing orb fell from its place above and broke in inky dark over the keep and village below like the yolk of an egg. The faint northern light went out, and I was henceforth forced to move solely by the light of the burning tree. These were no houses, I thought as darkness fell—they were sepulchers. This was no village at all, I thought bitterly—it was a cemetery.

¤

I met a girl named Spire at one of the ABC No Rio hardcore matinees, and after the show ended we took the long, long walk uptown to my apartment, like pilgrims to a shrine. It was still light when we left but long after dark when we finally arrived, well over a hundred blocks.

The entire time that we walked, we exchanged purely technical data. We started with music, where I first asked about the 1960s, the era in which most people my age in this crowd started hooking into specific bands or musicians (she loved the Beach Boys, on whom we spent twenty minutes alone), and then I followed the track forward decade by decade as the territory became more populated; when we had reached the current day, I transitioned to movies, which I handled using a similar system, exchanging dates, names, and directors; we had started digging into writers when we finally reached my block. We were both sweaty because it was summer and I hadn't suggested we take the train. When I saw the front door of my building I thought: *There, I've made it through another day without giving myself away.*

Inside, I turned on just the first interior light, like a torch illuminating the shadows of a cave. Spire went immediately to the window, which was the feature of most obvious value. The bathroom door was always shut. "You have a really good view," she said. "You can see the water." A delicate harp line lilted through the air: a peaceful river. I must have left my laptop playing when I'd last left the apartment.

We settled upon the long couch. Spire pulled her shirt over her head, and I lay over her. The sweat from her shoulders and neck spotted the upholstery, momentarily visible on the black surface before disappearing. The smell was heavy on us both, and we were already exerted so a part of it already felt done; if I had lived a hundred blocks further north I wondered if we could have elided the sex entirely, if the shared physical activity with another person would have been enough: eighty more blocks. Forty. I leaned in to kiss her, then blinked slowly before making contact and drew my face back. A line of sweat slithered past my ear. Her mouth was partially open, her eyes half-lidded; all of our responses were as if I had done it, as if I had completed the act and our lips had touched. I undid her belt and unfastened her jeans; her

154

hands did the same with mine. Our hands went beneath elastic into dark warmth at the same time.

I whispered, "Stop."

We paused there, my fingers beneath her underwear and hers beneath mine. The air grew dense and we held ourselves in that position, or I rocked minutely; though there was no broadcast movement, the points at which we were connected continued to react, and we grew wetter as a whole in the space of this pause, at the edge of this doorway. My breathing became sparser, I sprung a new layer of sweat and Spire did the same, and a coppery smell bloomed between us: again, it felt like our senses had progressed past our bodies, like we were much farther than we had planned to go, or like some part of us had eclipsed the bodies, had left us at the point where we, where I had to stop, but had taken the vision forward. A memory shivered through me. The back of my head prickled. Her thighs buzzed, alternately tensed and relaxed.

The bell on the front door rang. I froze, instinctively pulsed out another layer of sweat. Spire's eyes didn't move from mine: she didn't know what it meant.

A couple of seconds passed, and then I heard the sound of the outside door opening, and footsteps in the front hallway toward mine.

"It's my landlord," I said.

A series of seven knocks, in a deliberately playful pattern, ricocheted through the apartment and buried into my chest. I still grew hard in her hand, our warmth was still something we were maintaining, keeping close.

"So just ignore him," she said. "He'll go away."

"You don't understand," I said. "I have to answer. If I

don't, he'll just come in."

"What the fuck? Is that even legal?"

I withdrew my hand. "I don't know, it doesn't matter if it's legal, it's—he's my friend—"

It didn't make sense to anyone: it never had. And yet here I was trying to explain it, what suddenly felt like the most complex relationship in my life, but which came at a dire cost, the cost of this burgeoning one and maybe all others, the cost of living here, this friendship, this starving life that was everything to maintain, that was everything. "You've got to hide," I said.

"What the fuck? Why? What does he care if you've got someone in your apartment? Are you not supposed to be here or something?" She suddenly punched my shoulder. "Is this not your place, dude?"

It was too much, and I stopped hearing her questions: I no longer heard myself in them. She had let me go, but I was still reacting as if she was touching me; it was the familiar feeling of apartness, that my body wasn't mine but some arbitrary machine I'd been put in charge of operating, whose controls I couldn't figure out.

"Please," I said. "Just get in the bed. You don't have to hide, just can you get in the bed? Please."

She sighed and sat up on the couch. She walked across the room with her shirt, past the clock, and climbed up into the bed. She crawled under the covers and, with a scoffed exhalation, threw the sheets over her head. She was barely concealed—it was obvious that there was someone in the bed. I turned in the yellow light of the apartment; I made for the door as the knocks came again, a quiet call of my name, and then I heard him starting to enter numbers on the keypad.

156

I swung open the door just as it chimed to indicate that he'd unlocked it himself. As soon as the door opened, I realized that the smell was everywhere: ripe sweat, the haze of sexual activity just interrupted and still dissipating.

"Hey man, how's it going?" my landlord said, without indicating that he'd expected the apartment to be empty, stepping assertively over the threshold as if he still lived here. He held his hand up and I stepped into a hug; he patted my back and I patted his. I shook with the hand that I had just put against Spire and felt a surge of betrayal. I considered ordering him to wash his hands, immediately. I said instead, "Good good, man, how about you?"

He stepped back, now fully inside the apartment. The door closed with a click. He was dressed the same as always, like an off-duty fighter pilot. His shoes were perfect. His hair was in formation. He was responsible for everything; I saw his nostrils flare and knew that he knew he was responsible for everything, too, that I was interacting with him fully erect.

"Can't complain," he said. "Just stopped by to see if you'd got any of my mail recently? Got a Lexus RC for another thirty minutes."

Though I'd been living in the apartment for months, most of my landlord's mail was still delivered here. I toyed with the implications of the Lexus comment, whether or not it was meant as an invitation. I went to the cabinet whose top shelf was choked with his mail and deposited all of it into a plastic bag; the latest addition was seven identical envelopes with summons from an Italian traffic court. I thrust the armload of mail into his arms. I

157

imagined us in a penthouse somewhere, gleefully taser-
ing each other.

"Oh, did you want me to take a look at the ceiling in
the bathroom while I'm here?" he said, stepping forward.
I'd tied the bag, and it twirled from the single finger
in which he held it by the loop. It was now or never.
If he didn't see the damage firsthand, it would never be
repaired. I thought the light of the bathroom might dis-
tract him from the dark in the rest of the apartment: it
was not exactly the way he'd left it when he'd moved out
eight months before, but it was close.

I scampered to the bathroom and flicked the light
inside—it was fluorescent and antiseptic where the rest
of the apartment was a sickly, environmentally unsound
yellow; the bathroom was the only light I hadn't needed
to replace since my landlord left—and, together, we
looked at the ceiling. It was now bulging and buckled
in places, sagging and darkened with cystic reservoirs of
water. Little rivulets tracked through the plaster like pro-
nounced veins. I had taped two plastic funnels beneath
the largest and leakiest protuberances, connected to tubes
that deposited the water—which was yellow, though not
piss-yellow—into the shower. The sodden towels on the
floor collected most of the water that I was unable to
otherwise capture. A constant dripping sound accompa-
nied the bathroom now, and I kept the door closed to
contain the damp reek.

"Holy shit," my landlord remarked. Over the past
three months I had sent him maybe twenty photos of the
bathroom as it deteriorated. "I didn't realize how bad it
had gotten."

I flicked the light off quickly, as if embarrassed by this

black mark on the apartment that he had otherwise left for me, pristine.

I led him back to the front door, pulling the bathroom door shut behind me. The moldering smell followed. "Do you think you could have someone come in and look at it?"

I realized as soon as I said it that I had failed: he has already looked at it, I thought, and now this has created an additional step, another level of review.

"For sure," he said, too quickly. "We'll get Eric out here next week. If it's too big a job for him, we'll get a plumber."

Eric was the maintenance man. The job would be too big for him.

"And just make sure you create a ticket in the system."

I had no idea what tickets he meant, nor what the system was. I pictured the word *Narthex* on a white screen, a password I had no hope of knowing.

"How's everything else, man?" my landlord said.

In my panic, I accidentally strobed the second light once, momentarily illuminating the rest of the apartment. In the unexpected light, Spire squirmed on the bed; her foot, still in its shoe, emerged from beneath the sheet—a tenant!

"Dude," he said, dropping his voice like a friend, as if to keep it from carrying the twenty feet between us and the bed, "do you have someone here? Why didn't you say anything?"

I noticed that his hand was on my shoulder, but I hadn't felt it land there; I had missed the moment at which we had become intimate. I felt my eyes water. Why, why had I asked her to get in the bed? Why couldn't we have

159

stayed on the couch? What was I trying to prove to him, to prove to myself? What was I trying to trick myself into?

"Dude, I wouldn't have come in if I knew you had someone here. Text me next time, yeah?"

His hand was gone. I practically whispered, "I didn't know you were coming."

He was opening the front door. The implication didn't seem to have landed: his air was of a courtesy delivered. "I've got the Lexus for another hour."

He walked down the hallway—halfway down, it lighted automatically. I couldn't tell what he was asking or suggesting, if he was suggesting or asking anything, and I hated myself for noticing the disparity. I stepped out into the hallway, too, pulling the door shut behind me, as if I was going with him. He opened the front door, a hard ball caught in my throat.

"I'm double-parked," he said.

And then he was gone.

I stood in sight of the burning tree on the hill.

I followed the approximate path of the beast toward it in the darkness, the fire like a beacon as I navigated through the remains of the stone structures—the tombs—crouched in the dark. When I reached the base of the hill, my legs and back aching, my chest still smarting, the fire engulfing the tree brightened and then abruptly changed color, from yellow to gem-like blue. As if the tree had outlasted its prior physical shape and transfigured into something else, and so the fire could transform, too, could become whatever it was when it interacted with this thing that had once been a tree. I felt guilty, but also—I struggled to name the feeling—*accomplished* at the change I'd achieved, at the power of my impact. Maybe blue was what the tree had sought to be all along? Nevertheless, whatever the color, it offered light that I followed like a moth, and I sought to make as much progress toward it as I could while it was still burning, to put its random death to maximum use as a torch, hoping I could use its vestiges to survey from above, to plot my next move.

I stumbled up the hill, my bruises singing. As I climbed, the ground beneath my scratched and battered feet gradually changed from barren rock to thick snarls of petrified root. I realized that the tree's domain comprised a space much larger than just the outcropping on which it stood, in fact almost the entirety of the hill itself, and I doubted myself for a second, wondered at the magnitude of what the death of this tree meant for the ecosystem of this place, besides the practical fact that I'd been left almost totally disoriented.

Yet even as it burned into the firmament (or whatever was above me), it was hard to see the tree as dying, precisely, rather than merely assuming a revised form. The trunk—which I could now appreciate in some detail as I neared its cliff—appeared to be comprised of twined forms swept up together, nearly human in their shape—I saw arched backs and buttocks, the curve of a hip or breast or neck, maybe—like the naiadic forms you'd see at the base of a statue of Poseidon, figures all carved from the same hunk of stone. Above the trunk, the tree's many branches hooked into the air and sprawled in all directions, some so large and encumbered with other offshoots that they drooped and nearly touched the ground, but with all of the foliage burned off they looked more like human limbs, or at least took on their texture: they were toned and smooth rather than shaggy or knotty, broken only at natural angles, or at least angles that made anatomical sense to me. In fact, once the fire had stripped all that it could from the bark and gone blue, the tree continued to burn without noticeable effect, smugly, I thought, as if showing off its fortitude against the elements, its immortality. The smell of ash and smoke suffused the scene, and my vision wobbled a little; the tree flickered like an oasis. The fire undulated up into the air and assumed a purple color. My eyes teared up—that sultry tree. I ran my hands down my hairless sides to my hips.

I was just outside the perimeter of firelight, in the blanket of total dark that surrounded it—just beyond its sight—when my foot caught on one of the roots and I fell hard to the ground, face-first. My forehead banged another root, and I blinked out for a second.

I remembered the basin in the cave, and I realized that for all my efforts, I was no longer clean: I never had been. It was a joke that I ever could be. I felt the roots rubbing against my tender skin, the ash and sweat plastered into every crevice. I felt like I'd been spoiled, like somehow up to this point I had been scraping by under this illusion of purity, enough to participate in whatever was happening around me—holding my white gown up around my waist, shoes in hand as I tip-toed through mud, that was the image—but now here I was, down in the dirt and the dark like a hairless mole, and it was all bullshit: I'd never properly washed my hands, I'd fled from the keep, the tree was on fire, and I'd taken a wrong turn somewhere.

But still the tree spurted its aura out into the landscape,

those amorphous, genderless bodies swirled into it under the neon light, and running up against my hopelessness came the feeling that I was still a part of its system in some way, despite my lack of purity. I had made it all the way here, hadn't I? I had found my way in the dark, unworthy as I might be, and had supplicated myself at its roots. And did the tree not breathe along with me even as it vibrantly transformed, as we both strived for more? And I was positioned just so, lying here on the ground among the roots, a knot pressed beneath my navel, and my knees had found two furrows when I'd fallen, and there was a natural crook beneath the knot. The skin of the roots—rough like bark but smoothed over time, a resinous surface like that of a well-wrought staff—rippled across my belly, into my nipples. I felt my cock stiffen beneath me, as if the roots had activated it by proximity, drawing me toward this point. The flames shivered before my eyes.

I reached forward with my left arm, and my hand crossed the perimeter of light cast by the fire; my fingers turned a nightclub purple, and in that light it was no longer my hand. I turned the palm downward, and the light caught the valleys of shadow between the knuckles, drawing the fingers out—it was a fine hand. I was otherwise invisible, unwitnessed. My opposite hand sought purchase in the dark, and I rubbed myself against the knot, my cock jamming blindly somewhere into the root system below, the one hand held under the clublight, manipulated by the shadow, narrowing and lengthening. It twirled and spun like a dancer's. I clenched my buttocks and humped in the dark. The trunk of the tree twisted, straightened, as if the bodies I saw there were clenching, too, in response, pulling taut. It was not dying, not at all; it was growing, reproducing.

I shut my eyes, to savor the image, and when I opened them again, still bucking into the ground, the flames had gone green. The tree was now swarming; the trunk rippled beneath a column of flame as if through water, and the roar of the fire—where before I hadn't heard it, or had heard it as a mild crackling sputter like that of a campfire, comforting rather than destructive—drowned out everything else. I slammed my palm twice against the root I was using for leverage, like I was tapping out. I could see my whole left arm now in the green light, the muscles in dramatic shadow. I felt heat below me, around my crotch, not the receiving heat I'd heretofore imagined, but burning. It seemed to pull me deeper.

I smelled acrid smoke, like a slap, and I suddenly remembered awakening in the hospital to a nest of coiled black tubes hovering over me, belching smoke into the room. I was no more than ten or eleven. The terror was sudden and all-encompassing: I choked and coughed, my eyes stung and watered. The mass of tubes thrashed in the air, the smell fumy and noxious, like car exhaust, the heat of it blustering in my face. My body jerked instinctively backward in the bed, and I abruptly sat up, tugging my underwear down and causing the bedclothes to ride up the crease between my buttocks (the twisting, furious clouded shape had begun to resemble a face), and so mixed with the terror that had engulfed me immediately upon awakening, there was this stimulated point of shame, an almost ticklish hormonal surge, and the way those emotional currents twined with their physical manifestations colored my experience of that monstrous, snorting growth above the bed: it was like the grim after-image of pleasure, the oily black ball that pleasure coughs up in its aftermath, its chemical deposits—this was the bad runoff that was stored in your body, some-where. But in the moment, my instincts combined and systematically collapsed: I screamed, I vacated the bed, the flailing growth roared like a factory, like a laugh, and at the base of the tree, a sensory line ricocheted up from my cock to every part of my body that was touching the roots, finally reaching my sweaty, stupid head. I heard a loud crack, and this was what finally occasioned the long-delayed thought: *The tree is fucking burning down.*

I yanked the lighted arm away and shoved it at my crotch, thrusting frantically—as if I could stop it all, yes, by coming—and the next instant a massive, flam-ing branch fell just where my arm had lay. I shrieked; I came hopelessly into the root structure atop the hill, like a crotchal belch, and I shimmied frantically out of my crook on hands and knees.

Flushed with a deep shame, light-headed and dizzy, I climbed to my feet and stumbled back from the light, nearly falling again. My feet were leaden and hopeless. The tree split down the center of the trunk and crumbled at the same time as I saw, out of the corner of my eye, the bright spot of the fiery beast again, far below, ramming against some other barrier. It broke through, and disap-peared once more, leaving a smoldering outline of the hole it had created. I raced toward it down the hill before the glow faded from the wreckage as the tree behind me smoldered into ashes. I heard a chorus of screams, a yellow light splashed out past me, and I heard a soft voice on the breeze whisper, *Fucker*, but I did not look back.

◻

The internal doorbell rang, and I startled awake. It was 7:50 a.m. I climbed down from the bed and went to the kitchen sink to splash water on my face. If it was the internal door, it had to be my landlord, though he usually knocked. I resisted going into the bathroom; it was too big an ordeal now, and I figured I could last the duration of however long he was planning to stay. I didn't have time to feel resentful that he'd come by unannounced or woken me up. I wondered if he had already knocked and I hadn't awakened, if annoyance with me had prompted the bell. And there I was, awake for a minute and already sweating.

I went to the door and opened it. A short, elderly couple weighed down with cleaning products stood in the hallway. The man gestured past me into the apartment. I somehow knew, instantly, that these were my landlord's parents.

"Oh—he's not here," I said. "I think he's on 58th street."

His mother—a small, wiry woman with large glasses, a baggy green sweater, jeans and tennis shoes, her hair tied into a bandana, carrying bulging plastic bags—reached forward as if to embrace me, and I leaned instinctively toward her, baffled. She kissed the air near my chin and used the space and confusion created by this interaction to push past me into the apartment.

His father was a balding man of approximately the same height, also nearsighted, with a short-sleeved collared shirt tucked in and what I would call work shoes. He carried a mop under his arm and a bucket loaded with chemical sprays. "We're here to clean," he said, lifting his burden vaguely by way of explanation.

His mother deposited her bags on the kitchen table and flicked on the lights. I felt suddenly under attack, surrounded. I swiveled between the two of them, unsure who to address. "I don't understand—did my landlord send you?"

His father laughed and clapped me on the shoulder. In my dissociation at the physicality of the gesture, he edged into the apartment as well. His mother crossed the room and started to make my bed.

"Hey—you don't need to—"

"We'll clean everything," his father said, making a dismissive motion with his hand.

His mother gave her husband some direction in Turkish. He laughed loudly, shook his head, and started unpacking the bags on the table. He broke open a box of trash bags and ballooned one out. His mother rolled up the carpet in the center of the room and laid it against the couch. They spoke more in Turkish as his father filled the bucket at the sink.

"You don't keep your house very clean," his mother said. "Why are you still in such a small place?"

"I—I moved in here less than a year ago," I said, unsure why I felt the need to answer defensively, or why I needed to answer at all.

His mother opened the cupboards and made unappreciative sounds. When she opened the fridge—which at this point had accumulated so much old Korean barbeque from my landlord that it could scarcely hold anything else—she gasped and gave a command to her husband. He assented. She took off her shoes and socks, set them by the door, and donned rubber gloves.

His father felt for his wallet and keys, nodded at me, and then left the apartment. He used one of his wife's shoes to prop open the door.

"I don't understand what's happening," I said in protest.

"Sit down," his mother said.

I sat on the long couch, and his mother set to cleaning. She dusted the whole of the apartment in quick, furious movements while I watched, entranced and somewhat shell-shocked, unable to question her. When she had finished, she soaked the mop and ran it in a wide swath across the floorboards at the same moment that I remembered my phone on the bedside table, that I should get in touch with my landlord: he would be able to tell me what was going on. But the floor glistened like a lake, his mother moving assertively back and forth across it, and I felt stranded on my couch island, unable to cross. Music came from the phone speaker across the room: strummy guitar, a lonely flute. I couldn't remember what I'd been playing to help me fall asleep.

Sitting there mulling while his mother cleaned around me, I started to feel gradually that I was dirty in comparison, grimy like the apartment from my lack of a morning shower, and I needed to empty my bladder. But the presence of a stranger in my apartment made me profoundly self-conscious: I was wary of entering the bathroom and then emerging with her present in the same room, and besides the bathroom was so disgusting from water damage and incipient mold that I didn't want to risk her seeing it. I was embarrassed by the bathroom, by my landlord's failure to address it and by my own failure to convince him of his failure. Then his mother streaked across the door's threshold with her mop, and that option, too, became compromised.

"When are you going to get married?" she said.

Why did I owe this woman any answers? I thought to myself. Why should I care what she thought of me? "Next year," I said, to appease her.

She shrieked and clapped and began to mop more spiritedly. The music from my phone darkened. She asked me more brusque questions, and I answered them from the couch with my feet tucked under me, as best as I could, in similar fashion.

I weighed my priorities—getting to my phone versus getting to the bathroom—and the phone seemed the most immediately pressing. I tried to hold on to all the answers I was giving to his mother's questions; it felt important that I be able to relay this information accurately. When next his mother strayed to that side of the room, I gestured at the bed: "My phone?"

She scoffed and shamed me in Turkish. The mopping complete, she began scrubbing every surface. I watched the remaining water on the floor slowly evaporate in patches: there was a path I could take, like stones over a stream, to reach the other shore that comprised my bed and the nightstand. And my feet were bare, too—if she could traverse the wet floor barefoot without offense, then so could I. I rose from the couch, leaving behind a buttock-shaped sweat stain that disappeared like a waning moon behind a cloud, and I skittered across the apartment to the nightstand and picked up the phone. His mother did not acknowledge me.

I shut off the dungeon music. There were no missed calls or texts, so I opened my email, shaking for some reason, as if under heavy surveillance, to check and see whether my landlord had said anything, while the smell of bleach slowly rose to fill the air. There was an unread message my landlord had sent at 1:51 a.m. The subject line just read "flavor."

Before I could read it, there was a loud voice from across the room. My landlord's father had returned: in his arms he carried a pallet of pastries, and atop it two rotisserie chickens in plastic containers. "Where should I put them?" he asked. The door was wide open behind him. His mother answered in Turkish and motioned at the table. His father pointed at me. "Come. There's more in the car."

I blanked the phone, slid it into my pocket, and numbly followed. As soon as I stepped over the threshold, I remembered that I wasn't wearing shoes or socks—I would never be able to set foot in the otherwise-clean apartment again as-is—but then I resigned myself to the course of this absurd event.

Their car was a low-end Hyundai parked on the street out front, at least three generations and $30K less than anything my landlord would drive. The trunk was open and filled with Costco bags and bulk foods: more pallets of bread products, a twenty-pound bag of rice, reams of noodles, a forty-eight-can case of Diet Coke, an enormous platter of deli meat—more than a family of six could eat in two weeks, and almost entirely carbohydrates. Not a vegetable in sight. I lifted a single bag from the trunk, as if questioning whether it was all meant for the apartment, and my landlord's father shoved two pallets into my arms—one of assorted cookies, the other of croissants—and then a chocolate cake. I staggered back

170

inside.

When I entered, my landlord's mother had the fridge open and was opening boxes of Korean barbeque one by one, sniffing them, and then throwing them into a trash bag beside her. I laid the groceries on the table. "You need to eat better," she said.

"Ana is right," my landlord's father said, entering behind me with his arms piled high. "You need to be more healthy."

That was where I lost it. "None of this food is remotely healthy," I snapped, almost under my breath.

"Rice? White meat?" my landlord's father bellowed. "Which of these is not healthy enough for you?"

I pointed at the table. "There are like a hundred cookies there! Chocolate cake? What's healthy about that?"

His father held his hand to his forehead and said a Turkish word that I didn't know, but which I understood: *Enough*. "You can't talk to us like that."

"I didn't ask for you to come!" I cried in my pajamas and dirty bare feet. "I don't even know what you're doing here! I don't know who you are!"

His mother gasped, put a hand over her mouth. His father threw down the remaining bags and started yelling at me in Turkish, which I let wash over me in a wave of incomprehension, as if he were a stranger on the street—which I realized that he was, effectively—but the general tone of it was that I had disappointed and disrespected him, fundamentally. After some time, his mother cut in; the two of them spoke a while, and this seemed to calm him somewhat. I needed to read the "flavor" email to get in touch with my landlord—or I could call him, which I had never done before, only answered his calls—but I felt involved in his parents' conversation, even though I couldn't understand it, because it undoubtedly centered around me, and I thought it would be rude to interrupt it by looking at my phone.

An understanding was reached. His father took off his shoes, and the two of them continued to clean together, my passivity signifying some kind of agreement. His mother removed every decorative item from the shelves of the display case beside the bed and dusted them. I realized, dimly, that none of these objects were mine: they all belonged to my landlord, had been there before I arrived.

I looked away, embarrassed, and drew my phone out again. My landlord's email read, in its entirety: *hey dude – time for a quick favor? lmk.* My heart sank. What was the favor? Was I doing it now? Why couldn't he have told me in the email itself, and why email me at all with a last-minute request? Why not call? Why not text?

My bathroom needs were severe by now, and I felt on the verge of tears. His father wiped down the counters. His mother was examining the little hamsa she'd plucked off the shelf. I was sure that she recognized it as her son's. She turned to me, held it up, and smiled. I bit my trembling lip and smiled back, swollen with gratitude. She replaced it carefully on the shelf.

His father made a surprised and happy noise, and I turned to see that one of my landlord's huskies had padded into the apartment through the open door. I was dismayed, but bolstered; I assumed my landlord would be close behind. His mother exclaimed the dog's name and ran to embrace it. She rubbed its neck and kissed it while the dog drooled wantonly onto the just-mopped

172

floor. His father fell to his knees and joined in the petting of the dog, still wearing his rubber gloves. From the floor, he looked up at the large painting that hung above the couch, a cityscape at dusk with minarets, a distant smattering of ruins.

"That is a nice painting," he said, running one of his gloved hands down the dog's back. "I like it."

I choked again with pride, despite myself.

They spent what I felt was an extreme amount of time interacting with the dog on the floor, and when my landlord did not materialize at the door as expected, I grew agitated. Feeling both betrayed and ignored, and like the dog had somewhat spoiled my newly clean apartment, I took out my phone again and dialed my landlord.

He picked up quickly—too quickly, as if he knew. "Hey, what's up?" he said. His voice sounded different over the phone; it was a cliché but I felt as though I was talking to a machine, an entity who would not offer me the human help and understanding that I required.

"Hey, I think your—"

"Did you get my email?"

"Yeah, I just saw it. Look, I think your parents are here and I'm not sure what I'm supposed to—"

"What do you think?"

"About what?"

"About doing me a favor."

"You're not listening to me," I said. "Your parents are in my apartment *right now*. They're cleaning—"

It was then that I noticed his parents had forsaken the dog—who now lay fully on the floor—and were about to breach the bathroom door.

I crossed the room to intercept them, to keep them

from the bathroom, while my landlord continued to speak, to explain what was requested of me. I think this was the first time he'd mentioned the cabin, and I'm not sure if he acknowledged my complaints about his parents, or even that they were present. I babbled my assent over the line while broadcasting the opposite with my body against his parents—it ought to have been reversed.

Finally I hung up the phone, and his parents successfully shooed me aside and opened the door. A burst of fetid damp rushed out into the chemical clean of the rest of the apartment, but his parents didn't react to it. His mother turned on the light—revealing the bathroom's ghastly state—but proceeded inside, barefoot on the slimy towels, without acknowledging it.

His father followed, and swiftly, in tandem, they set to cleaning the bathroom as well. They rolled up the soiled towels and threw them away. They sprayed Lysol over every surface and rubbed them down. His mother stepped boldly past the dangling tubes and into the shower cube, where she attacked the glass door first and then scoured the tile walls. His father cleaned the toilet and the mirror and mopped the floor. Neither acknowledged the decay, nor seemed to take it into account in their cleaning. At times, their scrubbing came dangerously close to the discolored, bubbly patches in the walls that I knew were on the verge of breaking open, or to dislodging the funnels I'd attached to the ceiling. A new leak began and dripped brown water on my landlord's father's shoulder, staining his shirt, but he didn't appear to notice. When he finished mopping, he didn't replace the towels, and the leak dripped onto the newly clean floor instead, forming a puddle. His mother finished scrubbing the shower and wiped her forehead just as the ceiling finally tore silently open, depositing a thick stream of water over her feet. Oblivious, she stepped out of the shower, walked nonchalantly across the bathroom, turned off the light, and exited.

His father seemed to remember that I was standing there. "When are you going to get married?" he asked. "When will you learn to clean for yourself?"

I opened my mouth to give him the same answer I'd given to his wife, but she stepped in for me, shushing me with a finger. She spoke to him at length in Turkish—looking over at me occasionally as she did so, as if to validate what she was saying—conveying to her husband, in far more detail than I'd ever given her, the future shape of my life. And every so often, my landlord's father would look to me as well, asking with his eyes, *Is this true?* And I would meet them and smile—*Yes, it's true*—and he would smile in response and look back at his wife as she continued, and a picture was formed.

¤

I raced down the hill in the waning traces of light as the tree burned. I held in my vision the spot where I'd seen the beast disappear, the rupture in the wall where I too could enter: it was the faintest shimmer of light in the distance, like the artifacts of color that appear from staring at a light for too long, the air of an illusion or hallucination. I ran with abandon, without fear, as if the now nearly absolute darkness had also claimed any part of the landscape that could pose a threat to someone stumbling blindly around in it, had soaked every potential obstacle into unending flat terrain. I had lost all sense of direction. Phantom energy flew from my body, from the back of my head, the palms of my hands, the soles of my feet, my sticky crotch. I felt ash grinding into my thighs, into my armpits. Miraculously, I did not fall.

The fiery light behind me dissipated eventually into nothing, and I knew that the tree was finally dead. The jagged outline of the rupture in the wall grew closer.

When I reached the perimeter of the cemetery, the tombs began to block the passage from view, and my progress slowed. I wound my way around them in the total dark, desperate to keep that glimmer of smoldering light in my field of view, for I knew that it was dimming, too, going out, and I had to reach it before the door closed completely. Finally, I emerged from behind one of the tombs to find the glowing opening, ten paces ahead.

I climbed over displaced stone, still warm from the beast's passage, until I came to the mysterious edifice into which it had disappeared. Ahead of me, through a hole larger than I was, the beast had crashed through wall after wall of what looked like an old factory or workshop—a place of some industrial or mechanical use—blasting a tunnel deep into the structure. What little light there was came from wooden beams or other hangings that the beast had set ablaze as it trampled past, illuminating the chambers like makeshift torches. The sounds of further destruction, the beast's unearthly wail came from deep within, and the stone vibrated faintly at my touch.

I ought to have worried about the building collapsing, burning like the tree, but I didn't. I picked my way through the hissing rubble and climbed inside.

Corrupt iron machinery of mysterious purpose

176

surrounded me, grinding in error, casting spindly shadows across the floor. A punctured metal tank lay on its side in the center of the room, spewing steam into the air, saturating the room in hazy light. One of the busted pipes that ran the length of the floor pulsed out a rusty red liquid that spread in a pool like tainted blood. I became instantly sweaty from the steam, and the spilled liquid prickled the soles of my feet as I crossed the room—I was sure that blisters would form. I avoided touching the pipes. Everything around me bled heat: the rusted metal arms overhead, the dark cones above with their blown-out bulbs, the mammoth cylindrical vessels stacked in the corner, the archaic control panels and their smoking levers. The far wall was decimated—there had been a metal door that now lay discarded on the floor like a crumpled sheet of paper—and the next room was of a similar character, hotter still, with a grated coal furnace in the corner that the beast, thankfully, had not disturbed. Pipes ran across the ceiling here, too.

I crossed the room and stepped through the debris of yet another ruined wall. This third chamber was much larger and higher-ceilinged than the previous two, though the heat was just as intense. The room was octagonal in shape, and the same tortured-looking machinery occupied its perimeter, massive gears rutting uselessly against each other. Held aloft at intervals by crane-like arms were sleek metallic tanks, and the tanks formed a circle in the center of the room, maybe eight feet in the air, each with a tapered spout. The air above them rippled like a mirage; the heat in the room seemed to emanate from these vessels, fed by the connecting pipes and tubes that ran the breadth of the walls. They were intact save one, which lay on the floor: a bluish, waxy substance lay in a pool around it, already gone solid in the air. Corresponding to the silver vessels, in each of the room's many corners, a glass tube rose up and out of sight, each striated with the residue of a different color—yellow, red, green. Several of them had burst—from excess heat, perhaps—and left a faint splatter on the wall behind them. By the arrangement of the machinery and controls, which held the air of a fantasy foundry, I understood that the pouring-tanks could be manipulated and moved about: whatever was manufactured here was cast from the material they held. I couldn't fully make out the ceiling from where I stood—the way it glimmered when I shifted position, I wondered if some part of it was glass, if the ceiling had opened to the false sky beyond, before I'd blacked it out.

I had drawn these conclusions—that the room resembled a mechanized factory, and that a product was therefore made here—before I even noticed what was at the center of the room; I had, since entering this world of outsized places, or maybe since being born, automatically looked above and beyond me rather than in front. When I did finally look, I had difficulty piecing together what I saw.

At the center of the room was a raised, circular stone dais. The beast had obviously charged straight across it, as it was almost completely covered in debris. At the center lay the devastated remains of a pale blue human form, built from a substance that most closely resembled candle wax. The figure looked as though it had been mauled in the process of drying; only the top of the body was fully intact, while the center had been trampled through and melted by the beast, rendering the form's middle section

178

and its arms into a long, lumpy smear in the center of the dais, like a dead animal on the highway. The stiff, ghostly legs lay scattered on the opposite side of the platform, their ends eaten smooth and shapeless by the flames. The remaining top portion of the body—which started from the breasts up, like a bust—lay propped at an angle on the dais, seeming to stare into nothingness, at its own demolished lower half. The head was bald and the body naked, and the color matched that of the spilled tank elsewhere in the room, a ghostly blue. Symbols had been carved on the outer edge of the dais beneath the body: the outline of a cloak; a crescent moon; a pair of legs with cracks spidering through the pelvis, like those of a damaged statue. The symbols were lit from below and flickered like a broken circuit, then went out. The platform and mangled human form were streaked with ashy black residue from the beast. A process had been interrupted. I stepped toward the dais.

As I grew closer to the figure in the center of the room, I saw that the wax had not completely dried, as I'd assumed, but that the increased heat of the room—from the flaming beast, addled machinery, and influx of heat bleeding through from other rooms—had turned this room into a liminal space in which the wax could neither solidify nor melt completely. The bust of the figure at the center, the severed legs, the skidded puddle that comprised the rest of the body all held a wet sheen: intact, but still malleable. I knelt by the bust at the edge of the dais. Across from me, one of the symbols remained lit: a single eye, like that of Horus on an Egyptian scroll. I felt a little stab of surveillance, like my actions were being accounted for, the way that I kept fucking things up had started to take a cosmic toll, and this drew me to the empty eyes of the savaged wax form, blank and cast down. And though the face was bare, without clear gender, and the rest of the figure was obliterated past identification, I recognized some aspect there that compelled me to take the body into my arms.

Gently, I pried the bust from the goo that spread over the dais. The wax provoked the slightest resistance and then tore free, like wet paper, and for a few seconds I cradled the bust in my hands, as delicate as a web. As I examined it, the face flecked with ash grew more and more familiar, like trying to match a face in a crowd with someone I'd known years ago—I thought vaguely of my landlord—but in separating this part of the body from the rest, I had compromised whatever alchemical mix of temperatures was keeping it intact, and the wax began to soften and lose shape in my hands. The shoulders deflated in my palms like undried papier-mâché, dripping from my ashy fingers. I felt a desperate panic rising in my chest to save what I could; the forehead was marred with ash and I reached absently with my waxy hand to rub it away, but the crown of the head sunk beneath my fingers like a gum bubble, collapsing in on itself, drawing the browline upward. And only as the face started to shift away from familiarity—only once a distance was present where there had been closeness before—only then did the realization finally arrive: the face was mine. It was my face. Or it had been me, but it was me no longer.

The rest of the head lost form all at once, pouring through my fingers like warm water, drying on my arms, clumping on the floor. I raised my eyes to the shining vessels above me, rife with substance, to the swarming

180

heat they emitted, the action, and somehow I knew decisively that I could never make the conditions right again. The process could never be repeated. I let out a gasp, a little pathetic sound, and I turned toward the lower part of the body, as if to salvage something, some clue for how to be, but there was nothing in the mess left there to discern: it had long gone smooth and liquid, and the wax that had been the legs pooled and dripped into the symbols on the dais, settling permanently into the grooves where there was no way to clear it, to repair the damage that had been done.

Above me somewhere, I heard the call of the beast again, a pull of inhuman screams and commotion, then silence. In a dark corner of the room, edged in shadow, I saw a ladder leading upward, out of the factory. I stood and wiped my filthy hands on my thighs, leaving oily streaks of blue on my legs. I made my way to the ladder, and as I climbed away from the wreckage I'd made, I remembered a stretch of moments the year prior, two months before I'd moved to the apartment in Harlem, when I'd awoken at two a.m. in my basement room of the off-campus house I shared with five others, filled with the overpowering urge to leave the building. As I climbed the stairs, an unspecified anxiety building with each step—I knew only that I wanted to be out of there, that external air was the only thing that could unknot me—I saw through the open door at the top of the stairs an unfamiliar man standing in the kitchen. He was framed in the yellow nightlight, naked from the waist down, his penis erect, standing at the sink drinking a glass of water. And it occurred to me in the haze leftover from sleep that there was no reason to believe he wasn't an intruder, that he hadn't connived or forced his way into the house and raped one of my roommates and then, swollen and exhausted in his hormonal gloat, left them incapacitated or dead and gone to the kitchen to refresh himself, that if he'd forced himself on the house and the people within it, why wouldn't he feel entitled to a glass of water before leaving? And this casualness—this air that he belonged here, that it was his right to stand unperturbed and dicksore in the kitchen and hydrate—this was the most cunning deception, the way you don't question someone with a purposeful stride or who doesn't ask permission, who could walk into a home and take a cup from the cabinet and fill it, a bystander would think it was his house, his water, that he wore this disguise like the privilege of his veiny white cock in a gentrifying neighborhood, there was no reason not to believe this, and I was not fooled, and I bolted up the remaining steps and scattered him from the counter, his glass shattered on the floor, and my hand had grabbed a knife from the counter when Siobhan, one of my roommates, emerged from her room, and I misinterpreted her scream, too, and it was only a few seconds later—after I'd whipped the knife at the intruder once, twice, three times, unsure in the moment whether I'd connected—only then did I realize by the way their eyes met that there had been a flaw in my thinking. And as complex as the aftermath became in the months that followed, long after I'd left the house, I failed to convince a single person of my logic, which I thought plain, as obvious as the thick lines that separated one panel from the next in a comic strip. And the knot in my throat remained, or I didn't notice when it came undone, and when I reached the top of the ladder and climbed onto the platform waiting there

I was crying, because that was the only way of proving I was still human, therefore capable of mistakes, and I crouched through the little door when it was offered.

⌑

The bright and warm light was an immediate relief, but as I pulled the door open I was devastated again, my heart pulsed into my mouth and then sank all the way to my ashy, waxy feet: I was back in the council chamber in the keep that I had fled from, and the beast had been through here as well. The chimeric figures who had once sat at the table had all been slaughtered. The chairs around the table were empty or had been knocked over, and the bodies were splayed about the room in vicious carnage, their goblets spilled over the table and floor. Black, red, and faint pink blood streaked the floor and walls. The room was misty from smoke. The heads of the seven seated at the table had been smashed, burned, or torn apart, as if in sick vengeance: the fleshy flower now comprised a veiny pink mass at the center of a pool of shining blood; the knot of black coil lay unspooled like a swampy car wreck leaking oil; the marble-headed figure—the one who had looked closest to human, with whom I'd carried an instinctive sympathy—had been stamped indistinguishably into the floor like a bar of soap; the eclipsed sun was nothing more than a black scorch. Their golden robes had been mostly burned away, too, revealing the corporeal forms beneath: knotty gray armatures, like rudimentary figures in clay, molded by inexpert hands. They had no recognizable human anatomy, but were knobbed at angles enough to fill out the robes and approximate a recognizable frame, like a sheeted ghost, the heads and hands like movable elements of a puppet. As if they had catered their forms to me alone, and I, even as I'd fleetingly understood their intent, had become overpowered and run. I noticed the bird-head's feathered claw, smashed open like a shelled fruit, and it dawned on me: it wasn't the armatures that had bled, but the heads and the hands. It was the aspects they had fabricated for my small, mean eyes.

Something spiked in my chest, and I heard again the tree's whisper, *Fucker.* I wanted to step into the room, but I felt rooted there in the doorway, that terrible heat behind me, my failed self puddled in the factory below. And before me, the table now seemed clearly not a table at all but an altar, a place where a specimen—or better, an offering—might have been laid out and pondered, changed. It was a table at which I might have sat, and I had ruined it. I had ruined it all.

In my stupefaction, finally, I walked numbly into the room—the table's surface glimmered from the spilled goblets, a substance like red wine and honey mixed—and I took my smaller chair at the head of the now-empty table, at last. At each place, carved into its surface where the goblets had sat, I recognized the symbols from the dais where the wax figure had lay. I surveyed the devastation around me, the bloody mayhem of the room. Through the windows opposite, it was black; the tree, the last source of light out there, had long finished burning. I drank emptily from the dregs of the toppled goblet at my place.

I felt a burning on the crown of my head, above my ears. When I raised my hand to my scalp, to my disbelief, hair had sprouted. I ran my fingers through it—with one, with both hands—and it was unmistakable: there was a thin, fuzzy layer of hair where there hadn't been before. Where I'd been balding even before I shaved it all off, new roots had taken hold. I fumbled the cup to my lips again, craned my head back and held it, but there was nothing left. I dropped the goblet and scanned the table, but there were no more cups upright; their contents had already spread across the surface and mingled, run over the edges to puddle on the floor. I dipped a finger into the sticky mixture and put the finger into my mouth. I felt a glimmer of pain in my nasal passages, like the onset of a pressure headache, and I ran my hands over my face in alarm, down the bridge of my nose, but I couldn't tell if anything had changed. I inhaled through my nose, sniffed: the air felt slightly different as it traveled through, or it might have felt different. But now, of course, there was no way to compare with how it had felt before.

I hovered there for a long time, or what seemed like a long time: one part of me—the larger, basic part—wanted to devour everything on that table, to lap it up like a dog and see how I came out. Another part wanted to overturn the table, to scatter the spilled liquid and its potential into nothingness, to reject the choice I had been offered by refusing to allow that there was a choice at all, as if I'd never entered the room for a second time, or had only entered it hours later, when everything had dried to impossibility. I felt my head falling toward my chest before I acknowledged it, before I realized that this was the motion I was in—the pressure on my neck, the tightening in my jaw and the trembling in my throat, my brow furrowing, all like the effect of some other process, something taken from the goblets or hoped for—I was crying before I'd allowed myself to make a decision. And because the crying seemed to me like it was consequence rather than cause, I figured that, some moments ago, the decision must have already been made, I had made my choice, which was a lack of choice, which was drying on the table.

I heard a faint hissing close at hand, and when I got down off the chair I saw that it was the shattered bird-creature, not yet fully dead, its cracked beak straining to speak or call out, but I assumed—as it was a beak this one had formed in, a beak that presumably made bird-like sounds—that it was a language I couldn't understand, and I couldn't face this either, so when I heard the beast roar again, a foundation-breaking crash, somewhere in the keep, down the stairs, I turned and followed it through the wreckage instead.

¤

The door through which I'd entered the room for the first time was rammed open, the surrounding wall mostly destroyed. The comely statues on the landing had been toppled, too, and debris scattered down the grand staircase beyond, collecting against the arched door I'd ignored on my way inside. But the beast had not used this door. I picked my way downward through the rubble and, following the path of destruction and disintegrated carpet, the patches of charred skin, I eventually made my way back down that same winding staircase, now scorched black, to the cellar or underground prison from whence I'd come. Its close air now reeked of burning flesh, and I

186

stepped carefully through the warped and glowing iron bars—bent like plastic straws—and made toward the smoldering crater in one of the nearby cells. In retracing my steps from the council chambers above, the journey felt much shorter than it had on my earlier surveys: surely there had been more rooms, I thought, more meandering hallways. Surely it had been more complex than this. Surely there had been more turns involved than I was making now; I remembered a complex path, a labyrinth even, a series of dead ends and misdirections. It had to be more than one turn. It had to be more than a straight line.

And yet here I stood, above a crude hole in the floor, another byway, and I felt no doubt—like the pull of fate itself—that I should take it. A trapdoor had once lain there (a trapdoor which, I realized dourly, I'd somehow avoided noticing my first two times through) and the beast had stomped and battered until it gave way. Its remains opened into a wet stone space below, as if the beast had known or sensed where to find water, where to quell its pain. An earthy, damp smell wafted from the hole. A broken floorboard left alight from the beast's passage furnished me a torch—I spurned those on the walls—and I dropped down through the gaping floor into the darkened cave below.

I splashed into a foot or so of murky water, thrusting my makeshift torch up like a spear to protect it. I climbed up, wet and shivering, and traced my perimeter with the light: I was in a narrow passage that wound in two directions, bound by limestone on either side. Ahead of me—in the direction that I vaguely perceived led away from the keep—I thought I detected smoke, a trace of that acrid fleshy smell mixed with the air of the cave, so I chose to follow the river or channel this way.

I held the torch out before me as I wound my way through the earth, illuminating the space a few feet ahead, following the faint smell. The passage was wide enough that I could stretch my arms to either side without touching rock, where presumably the beast could have passed unrestricted. Occasionally, my torch illuminated another scrap of flesh floating on the surface of the water, like a path of breadcrumbs, or the residual charred smell bloomed from crevices in the rock where it had lingered behind, but I heard no further sound ahead.

I followed the channel for a long while, as the flame gradually blackened the floorboard, edging closer and closer to my fist. I remembered how the first time I had gone to my therapist back in Ohio, when I was eleven or twelve, I had endeavored to draw a map. We had begun our session on the couch but had moved to the floor twenty minutes in; he'd given me a drawing pad and one of his fancy pens to work with. At that time, I was spending my afternoons at home painstakingly recreating the maps from the appendices of Lord of the Rings on sheets of printer paper that I taped together. I always started precisely in one corner, shading in the Blue Mountains or the forests, but inevitably, in time, the map would become spatially confused or my sense of its proportions would skew: I would extend a mountain range too far in one direction, or at the wrong angle, or my little crown treetops would be too far apart, and the map as a whole would warp in its facsimile; I'd draw myself into positions where borders could never meet or where seas curved impossibly into land, and inevitably I would give up. I had started dozens of maps this way, trying to work from one corner outward, and had never got it right. But that forty minutes one afternoon on the floor of Robert's office, beneath a cloak of cigar smoke (which at the time I didn't read as smoke at all, but rather the innate scent of Robert's office, unique in the world), that forty minutes was the first time I had attempted a map without copying it from elsewhere: whether it was because I'd left the book at home or was anxious to impress Robert with my artistic skills, I don't know. I started in the corner, as I always did. He had a pad, too, on which he drew and took notes. As I carefully pulled out the spiky border and added a river, a patch of trees, random mountains, a collection of boxes that signified a village, Robert matched me, drawing his own map. I envied his movements, his light touch and long, swooping lines. It seemed impossible that he could ever make mistakes.

At one point the rocky wall to my right went smooth, the left wall vanished, and the air grew warm and wet, like hot breath. A dim orange light filtered in from where the space had opened. The water around my calves warmed, and there was another smell present where there hadn't been, a yeast-like tang that for some reason felt shameful, private, that I felt embarrassed to have noticed. It was as if the cave were breathing around me; I could almost hear it drawing in and out. I hugged the wall, cradling the flame with my naked body, until I'd crossed the area and the wall became rough again and the temperature balanced, never once looking toward the darkness on the other side, the distant glow.

"Do you talk to other kids at school?" Robert asked me.

I answered him without taking my eyes off the paper, reciting names, but I noticed him write it down on another page, some shorthand of what I'd said, as quick and careless a move as drawing a little tree. I felt the slightest tinge of betrayal. I thought for another moment, and then I listed another name: it was a kid in my class, Alan Watt, who I never talked to. I saw him note that down, too.

I answered more questions: I put castles in nonstrategic locations, little lakes in the middle of deserts where they surely would have dried up, deserts that flanked forests.

"Do you have a girlfriend?"

"I knew you'd ask me that," I said, with childish confidence, but still, a flag had been planted. I told him no, but I said "Not yet."

Even then, at the first session, I realized to some degree that I was playing a sort of game: Robert only knew the information that I gave him, or that he could glean from me in various ways, or from my parents. I liked Robert immediately, in time loved him, but there was no duty to report faithfully, and if I made my obfuscation slight enough, I learned, it would never be detected in the mess of the whole. The trajectory could be slowly, subtly changed. In the months and years to come, I would move on from maps to drawing creatures from Magic: The Gathering or Warhammer or videogames, and then to intricate, abstract designs. After each session, I would sit in the waiting room paging through old magazines while my parents spoke with Robert on their own in his office, while he relayed, presumably, whatever info I'd given him in the previous hour, tainting it in his own way. I heard

190

his baritone rumbling through the wall.

"What is the name of your land?" he asked me, during that first session.

"Simonthia," I said.

He turned his drawing pad to show me what he'd been working on: it was a map, too, with similar elements to mine, but it was much more detailed. Where my forests were blurry clumps with stems, he'd drawn collections of carefully spired pine trees, and there were roads connecting his villages with his castles in a way that made sense. My eyes bounded back and forth between his apparently effortless drawing and my tortured one, and I made a note to match his style. I wondered if he would notice if I added roads, too.

"Robertavia," he said.

The passage opened up in front of me. In the space of a few steps, both walls disappeared, and I found myself standing in a large, cavernous space. A cloudy light glimmered in the air overhead: I looked up and saw a line of torches strung along the distant wall of the cave, far above me. In the dim splash of light that the torches created beneath them, I picked out a dark structure against the same wall, a cross-hatching of beams that supported what looked like a narrow platform, mounted high upon the cave wall. The platform ended abruptly midway across the far wall, but followed the wall in the other direction until it wrapped out of sight. The torches continued in both directions along the platform, however, continuing past the place where the platform ended into empty space. If one were to stand upon that platform, I imagined, the torches would be mounted just above eye-level. They were designed for the person on the platform, not the one in the murky water. I felt as if I had entered this chamber by a path that was fundamentally incorrect, that I'd missed some obvious staircase or ladder or other cue. *One turn*, I said to myself. *One turn and I could be up there.*

I splashed into the cavern to try and further grasp its curious makeup. The water pulsed faintly around my legs. I tracked the line of torches that led away from the platform, turning to the left as I did so, and realized that they in fact described another path that branched out from this cavern, much larger and higher than the one I'd entered through. The line of torches continued down this passage—like a great hallway—as far as I could see, until an opposing string of torches eventually joined it on the flanking wall. Deeper within this passage, the walls no longer looked like the ruddy walls of a cave but like the smooth stone walls of a castle or some grand entryway. And sure enough, at the end of this extension of the cavern, a length I would have estimated—without knowing the true size—of at least a quarter of a mile, there was an arched golden door, cast in dramatic light from the torches. It floated in blackness at the end of the passage like a monolith. Even from this distance, I could tell that it was a door of considerable grandeur and that numerous detailed figures were carved into its surface, great elegant beasts from times of old; and yet, it was hopelessly beyond my reach. I looked from the golden door to the narrow crevice from which I'd slithered like an oily salamander, no more than a scraggly gap in the rocks, and I felt terribly bound to the lesser of the two.

I turned back to the cavern at large, resolved to finish what I'd started. If I could not reach the golden door— and maybe I had not been meant to, maybe it was a meaningless signifier or a decoy—then I would follow the torches as far as I could in the opposite direction, trying to find a way up to the platform. I trudged forward through the water to investigate the structure on the far wall in more detail, holding my floorboard aloft. The top half of my torch had crumbled at this point, and the flame now licked close to my fist, on the verge of snuffing itself out, and the water, too, seemed to have risen significantly: I was no longer able to easily walk through it, or more accurately wade, though it wasn't yet much above my knees. In any event, I made my way to the far side of the chamber, my light gradually illuminating more of the beams that supported the platform or walkway above. But I could see no ladder or other means of climbing up there. If I *had* wanted to reach that golden door, how could I have made it there from the end of the platform? I peered at the wooden support beams as if scrutinizing them for some hidden internal pattern; I eased my fingers lower on the floorboard-torch, so I was just clutching the splintery base.

My leg knocked against an object in the water, and my light illuminated a small wooden boat floating at waist-level, idling silently at the base of the wooden structure. It was just big enough for a single passenger, with a slat in the center as a bench. I saw the shadow cast by an oar stowed beneath the seat. But what was the point? Was there an exit to the cave some further distance ahead? Was I meant to take this boat somewhere? Fumbling around with my free hand, I found a rope tied to one end of the boat, leading upward. I surmised that the opposite end of the rope was tethered to the platform above. The platform—the boat—the water—the golden door. The boat was meant to bear me somewhere, clearly, but how to make the water rise? Was there a valve to release it? Ought I—

The flame from the torch nicked my fingers and, startled, I dropped it. The burning shard fell into the boat and rolled beneath the bench. In my panic, I reached into the boat to grab it, as if my fingers could extinguish the flame, but the moment I touched it I yelped and recoiled. I rinsed my stinging hand in the water, and by the time I had turned back to the boat, it had clearly caught fire. "You motherfucker!" I cried, splashing water over the sides of the boat in an effort to quell the flame. I repeated this for a space of time—cupping my hands, sprinkling water lamely over the boat—before I realized that it would be far easier to try to force some portion of the boat temporarily underwater. I applied my weight to one end, and the boat dipped, but the bottom scraped the ground—the water was still not deep enough to sink it, even a little. My next thought was to flip the boat and trust that water would get in that way, which I mostly achieved, but the rope was the impediment here—turning the boat over strained it, and when it successfully flipped I heard an evil groan both from the boat and, worryingly, from the platform above me. Now that it was finally upside down, having no way to verify that the fire was finally put out, I desperately threw myself onto the underside of the boat like a football player. I heard a sad crack, experienced a warmth in my belly, and then a troubling silence. I rocked quietly for a moment. Eventually, water belched into the mouth of the boat, I heard a loud hiss, and the fire was gone. I breathed slowly out, stood again, and righted the boat. It was still intact. I rested in the wake of my victory for a few seconds—not validated by my ingenuity, exactly, but that eventually my desperate flailing had prevailed.

Thinking that I might be able to better consider next steps if I was within the boat itself, after all that, I angled the mouth toward me. I placed one foot inside, and as I sought to steady the boat again, my foot broke through the weakened base, and water quickly filled the doomed vessel once again, scuttling it for good.

I extricated my leg from the debris and waded resolutely away from the boat, as if I'd hardly meant to bother with it in the first place: an incidental distraction. I continued following the line of torches along the cavern's wall and down the opposite passageway, away from the golden door. This passage was of similar height and span to its partner, but the walls were still cave rock, rough and untreated. I watched the torches along the platform pass above me; gradually, they blurred together, and I blinked them apart. I made slow progress, staring up at them as if transfixed, but these were the only lights left to guide me, or meant to guide some other version of me who'd entered from the opposite direction. They blurred again, and I blinked them apart, separated them like a chromosome. Together, and then apart.

I rounded the passage to the right, and then to the left, and then the light changed again, and my attention fell, at last, from the torches.

At the end of the passage stood the beast—or what had been the beast, for once I saw them, my perception shifted again. The figure stood now on two legs, facing away: the leathery skin or carapace had been entirely shed, revealing beneath it a body, so far as I could tell,

195

that was nearly human. From where I stood, the skin looked smooth and bleached of color, almost translucent, and the figure had thick dark hair that fell to below their shoulders. A spectral, bluish light emanated from their outline, illuminating the space around them. Astride the mask of hair, I saw the nubs near the shoulders that I'd noticed when I'd found them shackled in the stone house—the tomb—and they no longer looked like fresh wounds, but rather vestigial organs that had lost their use long ago.

At first, I thought the figure was standing before the crumbled mouth of the cave, that they had reached a dead end, same as me, and were unsure of where to go next. My stomach pitched in dread. But then, as I continued to walk forward—for I felt unable to stop myself from approaching, no matter the probable danger, because I had already followed them this far—I heard the faintest sound of moving water, like a stream over rock. I paused to listen, and after a moment traced the sound to the end of the passage. The mouth of the cavern was blocked by a great circular stone plate. And the glowing figure wasn't facing a jumbled pile of rocks, as I'd initially thought, but something that glistened in the ghostly light like flesh, some massive growth that blocked the door, letting through only the barest trickle of water.

My foot slipped against something in the shallows. I thought it was random cave debris at first and didn't look down, but as I walked forward again the debris multiplied, bobbing against my legs, and when I finally examined these shapes in the dark, I saw the sharp edges of scales, desiccated teeth, ridged fins: they were fish, the same species of ancient fish that I'd found at the top of the lake, or of the same family, and they were dead, too, dead and left to rot in this underground channel. The bodies seemed to fill all the space around me, their species as well as others, patches of scales and fat and jelly all matted together over time like soggy bread, a lifeless tapestry on the surface of the water. It broke silently apart as I walked through it, glomming back together in my wake. And as I neared the upright figure—who stood very still with their back to me, as if in study—the growth that they stood before became finally clear: a mound of dead lay piled at the base of the stone plate, clogging the mouth of the passage, keeping the great stone from closing completely.

As with the low tide at my legs, I couldn't discern one body from the next within the pallid mass, but I could tell that they were much larger, enormous, the same stature as the squid-like creature on the shore above, and that over time they'd been sapped of most of their color and shape, fused together into indistinguishable surfaces of skin and cartilage, bloated white flesh, oily sockets left from rotted eyes, pulverized innards, and thick coiled tentacles run with black veins. The glowing figure seemed to survey it all as I approached. I felt certain that they could hear me, and I begged for them to turn around and address me, to acknowledge themselves, to let me ask of them. I wanted it desperately.

When I was within perhaps ten feet of the figure, they lifted one arm into the air. I interpreted it as a sign telling me to stop, and so I stopped. I waited, in anticipation.

The figure reached forward and grabbed a chunk of the fleshy mound in their fist. They pulled, and the decayed body of some ancient aquatic animal began to slide from the pile, a listless tentacled thing. The mound slipped, and the sound of running water grew louder. The figure cast the carcass behind them effortlessly, then grabbed another tangled body and tugged. When the second creature was dragged from the mass—I thought it some bone-headed shark—a fresh stream of water pulsed out in its place, and the remaining pile slopped a little. The bodies began to shift against each other. I tried to move faster, but the matted dead around me were like mud, sucking at my feet. The figure cast the second creature behind them, and then reached out again, finding purchase. But still they would not look at me.

Water poured into the passage. I splashed forward as the figure pulled the third body aside. The mound began to collapse, and the water spouted from any space it could find. I opened my mouth to cry out, and only then did the figure slowly begin to turn toward me.

The lake exploded through the gap in the door, and the wave seemed to form in slow motion, traveling diagonally across my vision from right to left, like a curtain swept across a stage. For a long moment, I couldn't tell what was water and what was other matter, but I did remember, instinctively, to hold my breath. I was knocked off my feet, as if some giant hand had swatted my body into blank space, and when I came to, only a split second later, the water was noise all around me, like furious and endless static on a screen, lacking all sense of depth and proportion, and I thrashed blindly within it. There was the motion of my arms and legs pinwheeling underwater, seeking contact with anything, and in opposition, the surging current that tugged my body back and forth as the incoming water sought to fill the empty space, inciting a riot of opposing movement around my body, screwing me violently in place.

In the swarming black I found an arbitrary sliver of blue, a mark in my vision the shape of an eyelid, and I concentrated my every ounce of energy on making it to that space, to that narrow streak of color, whatever it was. When my searching foot finally struck rock, a crackle of warmth ran its way through my body—*structure, opportunity*. My limbs activated again, or I realized their potential use, and I kicked feverishly, grabbing at what I could, dragging myself forward through the churning water. I passed through a doorway. I heard, behind me, the sound of stone grinding against stone. I realized that before, in what seemed like an earlier lifetime, when I'd first found the hatch in the lake, the plate had been struggling to open, offering its unfathomable exchange; now, it was closing. And with the detritus, the dead piled at the mouth of the cave, I began to rise. The figure, I did not see again.

A woman approximately my age sat across from me on the bus. I didn't notice her specifically at first, for the bus was unexpectedly crowded when I boarded and people stood filling the aisle, so it was only after I'd been riding for a while and the aisle had cleared out—as the bus tripped from one little upstate town into the forested road that connected it to other little upstate towns, one of which, notwithstanding a two-mile walk, was my destination—that I noticed her, or she became revealed to me, or I singled her out among the remaining passengers, staring mutely into their phones. I'd been focusing on nothing, really, watching the landscape scroll past in the windows behind her, thinking shapelessly of my obligations in the week ahead, but then my eyes dropped or lolled, and I found myself staring at her. She had reddish hair that came down to her shoulders, was dressed casually in an umber-colored t-shirt and jeans, and wore headphones connected to her phone, which cleverly isolated her, allowed her to look around the bus—which she was doing—without any sense of intent. She didn't look in my direction—I was, for her, a part of the crowd on the bus, a point in the data of other passengers that would have almost certainly have vanished by the time she stepped off—but I lingered in hers, curiously. When I realized that I was staring, I broke my gaze away and made my eyes wander, too—I was also wearing headphones, but knew I couldn't achieve the same idle look—but, soon enough, I was drawn back. The thought seemed to flow through me like liquid, trickling down in a long shiver through my chest into my arms and legs: she looked, in some way, like me.

I writhed against the water, trying to propel myself upward through the eddy at the bottom of the lake, where the current rushed around me like a cyclone, acclimating to its new shape. I was exhausted. The pressure surged and drew back, popping behind my ears. I shuddered, and my skin prickled, as if I'd been exposed. But once I'd made the connection, I couldn't block it out—there was some common ancestry there, a shared lineage, as if we might have been distant cousins. And the longer I stared, the clearer and more obvious the connection became, the further I mapped my features onto hers: a Scandinavian heritage; the wide-set eyes; the defined cheekbones; the narrow, slightly upturned nose; the prominence of the upper teeth. Around me, the water parted colors. Dark shapes were moving with me, wisping past, years dead but held together by dormancy alone, now dispersed into faint clouds of flesh. Light spread like a spill. I was frozen in my seat, unable to pull my eyes away. I felt as if I was looking into a reflection, not of who I was, but of who I could have been.

She had finally clocked me staring, but I felt utterly unable to react. She glanced away, and then back at me, and eventually her eyes found mine. We seemed to lock into place, on opposite sides of the bus, rumbling beneath us. I shifted and uncrossed my legs; across from me, she did the same thing. I ran my hand backward over my head, the way I would have done with hair. My scalp was just starting to fuzz again. She matched the gesture.

I gasped as I broke the surface of the water. The sky was chalk-white and I blinked rapidly against it. I beat my arms to stay afloat. I heard splashing around me, expulsions of water as other creatures or parts of them broke the surface, jettisoned from the depths and pulsed toward the shores of the lake. I saw the cabin standing icy and alone on the hill, the gray remains of the squid on the shore in its benign desolation. I slipped below the surface again.

I blinked water from my eyes. She blinked in return. I felt a quaking in my body, a tightness in my chest. The similarities were there, it was unmistakable, but that was as close as I could bring myself—this matching game with a stranger. There was a distance that I couldn't cross, that I didn't even realize existed, let alone understand could be bridged, where I balanced trembling at the cusp. I was borne forward, among that tide of prehistory, of things that couldn't—I couldn't—flushed out alongside the world's defunct and outmoded forms, rising from the center.

It was who I should have been.

I laughed, dissipating the moment. I raised my right arm in a half-wave. She followed suit, adding a partial salute with two fingers. We laughed together. Within a minute, our interaction had ended.

My head dipped in and out of the water for the hundredth time. I swallowed air. My toes grazed rock. The sky shifted again above me, filtering the lake a shade darker. The bus wound slowly through the hills, rising and sinking as I sat motionless, watching for change. What possibilities lay within me yet?

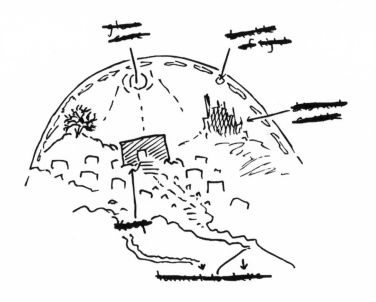

ACKNOWLEDGEMENTS

The earliest story in this collection dates from 2012, when I was twenty-one, and the latest I'm just finishing now, so as a result this collection encompasses several distinct stages of my adult life.

First and foremost, I have to thank Jeanne Thornton and Miracle Jones, co-publishers of the darkness (and Instar Books), who are each indefatigable cheerleaders, visionary artists, and inarguably Good Souls, and who with their own work have cracked open my writing in ways that I could never have expected. They have each shown extraordinary care and patience with this collection since way back in 2015, when it had a different, less genuine title and was comprised of totally different stories (only one remains).

Thanks are especially due to Jeanne, who has been a spirited collaborator, brilliant editor, and trusted friend in ways that go far beyond this collection ever since I read *The Dream of Doctor Bantam* and snuck a four-panel comic into her Austin monthly *Rocksalt* in 2012.

I also have to give enormous credit to *Paper Darts*. "Masterworks" (the story cycle) was first published in installments via the *Paper Darts* newsletter between 2014 and 2017. I'm grateful to Holly Harrison, who shepherded this weird idea into the light, and to the peerless Alyssa Bluhm. Alyssa took over the series midway through (at the octopus), and thereafter guided the story, over several years, into new terrain that became much more than the sum of its parts (and whose clear-headed judgment, sharp insight, and impeccably selected gifs I have come to depend on, as one does water or air).

I'm grateful as well to *Paper Darts* co-founder Meghan Murphy, a magnificent artist who was a part of this collection from its very inception, and whose work has been a longstanding influence. *Paper Darts* is among the best out there, and has been one of my guiding lights since I started reading fiction on the internet.

Thank you to my family, who has given me my sensibilities: my parents, grandparents, and obviously my brothers Eli, Michael, and Jack. They are all over this book.

Thanks to Sam Skurdahl for being funnier than I am. I admit it.

Thanks to Graham Nissen for his manifold influence and inspiration over the past decade, and for the collages that hang on this book's website.

Thanks to John Baren, Joey Holloway, Lindsay Hunter, Eric Kranz, Elysse Preposi, Tyler Pry, Amber Sparks, Ross Wagenhofer, Brandi Wells, and Chad Wells.

I'm also grateful to the editors of the other publications in which some of these stories appeared in earlier forms: "Let Me Take You to Olive Garden" in *Joyland*; "The Histories" in *Tin House*; "Secret Message" in *Paper Darts*; and "Partners" in *SmokeLong Quarterly*.

Simon Jacobs
March 2019, NYC

ABOUT THE AUTHOR

Simon Jacobs is the author of the novel *Palaces* (Two Dollar Radio), and of *Saturn* (Spork Press), a collection of David Bowie stories. He is from Dayton, Ohio, and currently lives in New York City.

ABOUT INSTAR BOOKS

INSTAR BOOKS publishes electronic and print literature, embracing contentious new models, welcoming the creative chaos of a destabilized industry. In addition to ebooks and paperbacks, we are intrigued by the possibilities of texts as social destinations, as performance, and also as digital sculptures, or "seeds." In fact, we want to try every goddamn thing.

We do not believe that genre distinctions are meaningful. Novelists and poets do not want to work for massive media conglomerates or make more bricks for giant corporate hell-castles. Readers do not want their literature mediated by marketing executives trying to build inoffensive global brands. We offer an alternative, unconvinced that readers and writers must only choose between old media incompetence or new technology relentlessness in order to consume and produce great work.

More information, including our complete catalog and ordering information, is available at http://www.instarbooks.com.